THE Princess OF Neptune

Also by Quentin Dodd

Beatnik Rutabagas from Beyond the Stars

QUENTIN DODD

THE Princess OF Neptune

Farrar Straus Giroux / New York

www.fsgkidsbooks.com

Library of Congress Cataloging-in-Publication Data
Dodd, Quentin, 1972–
    The Princess of Neptune / Quentin Dodd.— 1st ed.
        p. cm.
    Summary: Middle-schooler Theora Theremin and her brother Verbert find
themselves whisked from the shores of hometown Lake Philodendron to an
intergalactic beauty contest on Neptune.
    ISBN 0-374-36119-3
    [1. Outer space—Fiction. 2. Brothers and sisters—Fiction. 3. Beauty
contests—Fiction. 4. Bands (Music)—Fiction. 5. Science fiction.
6. Humorous stories.] I. Title.

PZ7.D66275Pr 2004
[Fic]—dc22

                                                              2003060671

To Charles

THE Princess OF Neptune

1

"**M**iss Theremin?"

I jumped. Mr. Pinweed was staring at me. So was the rest of the science class.

"Well?" Mr. Pinweed asked.

I had no idea what the question was. I had been thinking about a microphone.

I play drums in a band, and most of our equipment is secondhand, which means that it's always breaking. Yesterday our microphone had stopped working, and I was wondering what we were going to do if we couldn't fix it, when Mr. Pinweed called on me.

"Theora, your topic?"

Then I remembered. The science projects. The science projects that were going to be half of our semester grade. Today was the day we were supposed to tell him what our projects would be about. It had completely slipped my mind.

"Umm . . ." I said.

"Yes?" Mr. Pinweed made a big show of straightening his

bow tie. He always does that when he's waiting for someone to give him an answer.

"My project . . ." I said, stalling for time.

"I have given you ample warning about this, Miss Theremin. Ample warning."

"I know, I know." I tried to think fast, searching my mind for anything that sounded scientific.

"I'm going to do my project," I said, "on Big Phil."

Mr. Pinweed raised one eyebrow at me. "Miss Theremin, while it is impossible to prove a negative, which is to say that no one can say with certainty that Big Phil does *not* exist, it is the opinion of every educated person in this town that Big Phil is a fiction created by our unscrupulous chamber of commerce to serve as a centerpiece for the Phil Phestival."

The Phil Phestival is our annual summer carnival here at Philodendron Landing. It lasts for a week and has rides, a beauty pageant, a car show, regular festival stuff. The main event is the regatta, where people come down to Lake Philodendron on Friday afternoon and put their boats in the water. Then this huge fleet, which has everything from antique sport sailers to junky old bass boats, sails in big circles around the island in the middle of the lake. The official purpose is to search for Big Phil, the monster that's supposed to live in Lake Philodendron, but it's really just an excuse to drink beer and show off your boat.

4

"Ever since the Indians lived here, there have been reports of a giant creature in the lake," I said.

Mr. Pinweed was not convinced. "It is now commonly believed that the Indians were trying to frighten the settlers into settling someplace else, and made that story up."

"It's possible, though, isn't it? I mean, everyone thought the giant squid was a myth, but then they found those."

"You have a point." Mr. Pinweed looked like he'd eaten a bad peanut. "But I'm going to want a serious project from you. I don't want you sitting by the lake for four weeks and then writing a report that says 'No monster.' I want to see a rigorous application of the scientific method."

"You will."

"I'd better," he said, writing in his grade book. "Theora Theremin—the creature of Lake Philodendron."

When class ended, I was walking down the hall, trying to think of a way to apply the scientific method to a lake monster that may or may not exist, when Mary Beth Montengo and Ginger Norton came up behind me.

"Did you notice?" asked Mary Beth. "Dylan McMasterson looked at me in class! I turned around to pick up my pencil, and there he was, looking at me!"

This was hard to believe. To Dylan McMasterson, Mary Beth was probably no more real than Big Phil.

"I saw it, he looked right at her," Ginger said. "Well, at least he looked *near* her."

I sighed. "He sits in the back row," I reminded them. "He has to look *near* you to see the teacher."

"I know what I saw," said Mary Beth.

"Okay." I wasn't about to get into this for the thousandth time. "Do you mind if we skip practice today? I really ought to get down to the lake and figure out what I'm going to do with this stupid science project."

Ginger and Mary Beth were the other two members of my band. Ginger played guitar and Mary Beth played bass. All of us took turns singing, depending on who knew the words. We didn't have a name yet, and it was possible that we never would. I wanted something short, like L7, Ginger wanted something girly, like the Eyeliners, and Mary Beth wanted the Mary Beth Montengo Band. Every time we tried to decide on a name we ended up not speaking to each other for days, so we've learned to live without one.

We rehearse in my parents' garage, when I can get one of them to move the cars. Mary Beth's and Ginger's parents don't tolerate punk rock as much, so they tend to get pale and chase us out when we try to practice at their houses.

I think we're starting to sound pretty good. Obviously, we've got a long way to go, but we can get through most songs without stopping now. We even had our first gig a couple of weeks ago. We played at Cindy Gabriel Rossetti's birthday party, and almost everyone stayed through the entire set of songs. That's progress.

"No problem," said Mary Beth. "It's going to take me another day to see if I can rewire the mike anyway." Her dad owns an electronics repair store, and she knows all about fixing things. With the kind of equipment we have, this is just as important as her bass playing.

"She's only saying that so she can stay home by the phone," said Ginger, pretending to be serious. "Dylan might call."

Before Mary Beth could respond, a locker door slammed shut in front of us. Behind it was my brother, Verb.

"Hi, Theora! Hi, Mary Beth! Hi, Ginger!"

"Get to class," I said. Verb is a couple of years younger than me, and as far as little brothers go, he's not terrible, but that isn't saying much. He's certainly better than Ginger's brother, who I suspect was the one who broke our microphone, but Verb's not above poking his nose in where it's clear he's not wanted.

"What were you talking about?" he asked.

"Nothing."

"Were you talking about Randy McMasterson's brother?"

"None of your business," I said.

"Do you know Dylan McMasterson?" asked Mary Beth.

Verb blushed, like he always does when Mary Beth talks to him. "Kind of. Well, a little. I could find out more, if you want me to, Mary Beth."

"Out of the way, Verb, we've got to get to math." I detoured around him and headed for my next class, still thinking of what to do about Big Phil.

$$2$$

Smersh Memorial Junior High isn't far from my house, so it usually takes me only fifteen minutes to walk home. Today, I made it in five. I let myself in the back door and rushed upstairs to my room. I started changing clothes, trying to be as fast and as quiet as I could.

I wasn't quiet enough, because my mom called up from downstairs. "Theora! Is that you?"

"Yes!" I shouted into the air vent. "I'm just leaving! I've got to go down to the lake! Science project!" I got out of my school clothes and into the jeans and T-shirt I use for skateboarding. That way, Mom wouldn't freak out if I came home muddy from sitting on the shore.

"Take your brother with you!"

"Do I have to?"

"It would be nice. He likes to go places with you."

"But he's not here yet. If I don't leave now, I won't have very much time to, um, do my science things."

This was exactly why I had hurried home when I saw Verb talking to some friends of his after school. Verb lives to follow me around, and if I could get out of the house before he got home, I would be free of him for the whole afternoon.

I dumped my backpack out on my bed and threw in my binoculars and an old notebook. I kept my Keith Moon signature drumsticks. I never go anywhere without those.

"Gotta go!" I yelled, running back down the stairs. "See you later."

"What kind of science project are you doing at the lake?" Mom asked.

"You know, animals and stuff." I grabbed my old boots from the back hall.

"Well, take your jacket."

"Okay," I said, not doing it.

"Be careful. And be home in time for dinner. It's clam night."

"You bet." Then I was out the door, on my bike, and safe.

Lake Philodendron was created by glaciers, and it's a pretty big lake. You can stand on one side and just barely see all the way across. Dad always says, "It's not a great lake, but it's not too bad." He thinks that's hysterical. I don't know why. Part of the shore is a state park. There are a lot of big fancy houses along the northern side, and the Grand Philodendron Hotel sits over by itself on the far edge. This is the part I like best. It takes forever to ride out there, but I don't mind.

The Grand Philodendron was a really famous hotel back in the 1920s, and they say that Al Capone and a bunch of other gangsters used to come up from Chicago and stay there. Once the gangsters all got sent to jail, the hotel started to go downhill. It's been abandoned for years and years, but recently someone bought it and has been working on restoring it.

The restorers' trucks had worn tracks in the overgrown gravel road that led through the woods to the hotel. I followed the tracks part of the way, then pushed my bike into the bushes and walked to the edge of the water.

I found a spot on a boulder that jutted out into the lake, between a young black alder and a peach-leaved willow tree, and sat down. Mr. Pinweed was big on botany, so I knew the names of all the local plant species. Every week, Mr. Pinweed took us down to the little greenhouse behind the school building and made us work on the cactuses he had growing there, while he lectured to us about plants. I always suspected that he wasn't really interested in teaching us anything, he just wanted the cheap labor. We had to monitor the soil moisture level, record the growth rate, check for fungus, and repot the plants when they got too big. It was hard work. We were pretty sure he liked them more than he liked us.

I took out my notebook and wrote "The Creature of Lake Philodendron" across the top of one page. I knew my project had to use the scientific method. Mr. Pinweed was a nut about it. Almost every other day he would say, "If you aren't using the scientific method, you're not doing science. You're just doing stuff."

Since he wasn't wild about my project idea to begin with, my best hope for a decent grade was to be extra-scientific. I wrote "Hypothesis" in my notebook. When you're using the scientific method, you start out with a hypothesis, which is just another name for an idea. I wrote: "A large aquatic animal of some kind, commonly known as Big Phil, lives in Lake Philodendron."

I chewed on the end of my pen for a while, which is a habit my mom hates, and watched the ripples in the water. Once you have a hypothesis, the next step is to think about how you can prove or disprove it. I wrote: "Step One: Observe the lake and note any occurrences that could indicate the presence of a giant creature." A fish broke the surface of the lake and disappeared with a splash. Minutes went by. Nothing happened.

I got out the sticks and started to practice my part from "Gee Angel," my favorite Sugar song. More than anything else, I wanted to be Malcolm Travis. Before that, it was Bill

Ward from Black Sabbath, and before that, Mickey Dolenz from the Monkees.

As I played, and watched the water, I started to get a sinking feeling. This was pretty close to what Mr. Pinweed had warned me about. Maybe I could go back tomorrow and change my topic.

"Theora!"

I didn't even need to turn around to know who it was. I kept drumming on the rocks. "Go away, Verb."

"You're not supposed to be out here, Theora. Nobody's allowed out by the old hotel." Verb pushed his way through the brush to get to where I was sitting. Once again, my brother had found me.

"I saw you riding off when I came home," he said.

"Does Mom know you're out here?"

"She said I could."

"I don't believe you. Go home, Verb."

"But I want to stay here," he whined. He always whines when I tell him to go away.

"I have to work on my science project. You'll bother me."

"I can help. I got an A-plus on my solar system test today. I even got the extra credit. Nobody else in class knew what the Oort cloud was."

"I'm not interested in the solar system."

"Come on, please?"

I didn't say anything. I was staring out at the lake. About twenty yards offshore, the water was starting to foam and bubble.

"Mom always says—"

"Shut up, Verb."

Verb noticed what I was watching, and got quiet. Even in normal circumstances, that would have been pretty amazing.

"What is that?" he whispered.

"I don't know."

The bubbles got thicker, and then a huge gray shape heaved itself up out of the depths.

As we watched, the gray shape became a round dome. We stared at it. It was silent. All I heard was the gurgling of the water and the far-off sound of a bird. The gray thing got larger, rising farther out of the water.

This was just my luck, I thought. I say I'm going to do a science project on Big Phil, then I actually see the creature, and I don't have a camera.

A bank of yellow-lighted windows appeared above the water. I sat back, feeling disappointed. It was just some guys in a submarine.

Still, it was a submarine, which is pretty unusual for Lake Philodendron. I couldn't imagine how these people, whoever they were, had managed to get something this big and strange into the lake without its at least getting a mention in the *Daily Bloom*, our local newspaper.

It bobbed there on the surface for a minute or two, then a hatch sprang open. A head and shoulders appeared. It was a person wearing an elaborate wet suit and high-tech goggles that covered the whole top half of his head. He noticed Verb and me standing there. He looked at us. We looked at him.

The person shouted down the hatch. "Melvin! Did you check the scanner?"

"Yes," answered an echoey voice from somewhere inside the submarine.

The person in the wet suit looked at us again, then yelled back down to Melvin. "There are people out here," he said.

"The scanner says there's no one around for miles," replied the voice.

"There are two people on the shore right now. They're staring at me!"

"I don't know what to tell you. That's not what the scanner says."

"Melvin!"

Verb waved at the man in the wet suit. He waved back.

The man's shoulders drooped a little. "All right, bring her in," said the man, and the submarine started to cruise toward us. As it got closer, the man took off his goggles and pulled back the hood of his wet suit.

Verb gasped and clutched my arm. "Do you know who that is?" he asked me. "That's Dr. Jonathan Übermind!"

"Impossible," I said, prying off Verb's hand. "What would a famous scientist be doing here?"

"Look!"

The submarine reached the shallows at the edge of the lake. It continued to come closer until we could hear its underside scraping against the rocks, and then it stopped. The man climbed out of the hatch. He slid gracefully down the curved side and landed in waist-deep water.

The man really did look like Dr. Jonathan Übermind. Maybe Verb was right.

"Hello," he said. "I'm Dr. Jonathan Übermind. You may recognize me." He was tall, and his gray hair was perfectly brushed. He took a pair of horn-rimmed glasses out of a pocket in his wet suit and put them on. Now he looked exactly like he did on the back covers of his books.

Dr. Übermind was the head of the Übermind Institute. From its headquarters on an island off the coast of Maine, he and his team of scientists traveled around the world, investigating mysteries and solving people's problems. They published books about their adventures, which were all best-sellers. Verb had the complete set. He read and reread them, going through at least one a week.

"Theora, give me your pen! Give me your pen! I want to get his autograph!" Seeing his hero in real life had put Verb into a frenzy.

"All right, fine," I said, handing it over. "Just don't drop it in the lake, okay? It's the only one I've got."

Dr. Übermind grabbed a low-hanging tree branch and pulled himself up to where we were standing.

"No need to worry about pens," he said. "Here you go."

Dr. Übermind took a card out of his pocket and handed it to Verb. It had an abstract drawing of a giant brain printed on it in purple ink. This was the Übermind Institute's logo. Under that was the motto "Knowing Things Is Good." Dr. Übermind tapped the logo and his signature appeared on the card, as if it had been written in invisible ink.

"Übermind Instant Autograph," he said. "These cards are keyed to my individual bioelectric patterns. It's such a time-saver, and so much easier than always trying to find a pen."

"Hi," I said. "I'm Theora Theremin."

Dr. Übermind shook my hand. "I am very pleased to meet you. And who is this?" he asked, looking at my brother.

"Verbert Theremin."

I was impressed. Verb never tells anyone his full name.

"I've read all your books," said Verb.

"Thank you very much. That's very intelligent of you."

"Theora hasn't."

I shot a look at Verb. "I like your books, too, Dr. Übermind," I said. This wasn't exactly true. I had read a couple of them from Verb's collection, but they weren't really my kind of thing. It didn't seem polite to say that, though.

My brother was still staring at Dr. Übermind. "I can't believe it," he said. Then he frowned for a second, leaned forward, and poked Dr. Übermind in the ribs.

"Ouch," said the scientist.

"Verb, poking people is rude," I said.

"Sorry. I just remembered your book *The Adventure of the Mayan Manhunt*, where you used holograms of the Übermind team to distract the ocelot smugglers."

"I'm not a hologram," said Dr. Übermind.

"I know," said Verb. "Now."

Dr. Übermind looked at Verb, then at me, then back to Verb. "Although I am very pleased to meet you both, this does present something of a problem," he said.

4

"**Y**ou see, Melvin and I are not really here," he said.

Verb wound up for another poke, and Dr. Übermind took a step backward.

"What I mean to say," he said, slipping on the wet rocks and almost losing his balance, "is that no one is supposed to know we're in the area. We are working undercover."

He unzipped his waterproof wallet and handed us a plastic ID card. It had Dr. Übermind's picture on it, and the seal of Miskatonic University. Under the picture was the name "Bart Escobar, Adjunct Professor of Marine Biology."

"Melvin and I are here on a preliminary research mission. There are legends of a large, dinosaur-like aquatic creature in this area, and I wanted to investigate for myself before beginning a full-scale Übermind Institute project. When you're a famous researcher like me, it's hard to get a lot of real work done without being interrupted. So we are traveling incognito."

I was about to say that I thought they were traveling in a submarine, but I stopped myself. This was the first time I had met a famous person, and I didn't want to spoil things by making a stupid joke.

"So you see why I am concerned that you found us," said Dr. Übermind. "There is an apple in the sub that I was saving for my lunch. If I gave it to you, I don't suppose you would pretend you never saw us?"

"Probably not," I said, nodding toward my brother. In my entire life, I couldn't remember Verb ever keeping a secret. It's just not in his nature. He learns things and he wants to share them.

"Are you sure? It's a specially cultivated apple. It's two feet wide." Dr. Übermind looked hopeful for another second, then he seemed to accept that he was stuck with us.

He called to the submarine. "Melvin! Go on back to base. I've got some thinking to do. I'll walk along with these young people. And be sure to overhaul the scanner when you get a chance."

"I'll put that on the list," said Melvin, from inside.

The submarine pulled back into deeper water, then cruised away, staying close to the shore. Dr. Übermind followed it, walking along the rocky edge of the water. We followed him.

"If I may ask, what were you doing around this part of the lake?" said Dr. Übermind. "My charts tell me that this side is uninhabited."

"I was searching for Big Phil," I said.

"Pardon me?"

"The creature of Lake Philodendron," chimed in Verb. "I was helping."

"Not exactly. I was working on my science project," I told Dr. Übermind. "Verb was tagging along."

"I was not!"

"Yes, you were."

"In any case," said Dr. Übermind, stroking his beard, "it is encouraging to meet fellow scientists working in the same field. Tell me, have you seen anything?"

Verb answered first. "Not yet, but we're still observing the area. It might be easier if we could use your mini-sub."

"This is my first day," I explained to Dr. Übermind. "I was only here for twenty minutes before you showed up."

"We have been inspecting the depths of this lake for a week now," Dr. Übermind said, "and we have found very little indication of giant creatures. That being said, however, we did observe a school of suspicious bluegill, and I am almost positive that we encountered a pike that wanted to tell me something. I'll have to check the videotape."

"So there's no monster in the lake?" I asked. This wasn't good news. If Jonathan Übermind himself couldn't find any monster, then my science project was in trouble.

"I believe it is too early to make that kind of state-ment. After all, it took me three expeditions before I could document and classify the legendary Giggling Eels of Scotland."

"*The Mystery of the Laughing Loch!*" said Verb. "The adventure where you had to outwit Hondo MacAddersly, the Mad Biologist of the Highlands."

"Three expeditions?" I repeated. "Maybe I should go tell my teacher that I'm going to grow bean plants under artificial light."

"You can't grow plants," my brother said. "Remember when you poured hot tea on Mom's plants and they all died?"

"That wasn't my fault. Mom said we could put tea on the plants. I didn't know she meant tea leaves." For the millionth time, I promised myself that the next time I caught Verb doing something stupid, I would never let him live it down.

We were getting close to the Grand Philodendron Hotel. I could see a white panel truck, like a moving van, parked in front of the hotel's garage.

Dr. Übermind cleared his throat. "I've been thinking about our situation, and I believe I have an answer. I know it's not every day that you get a chance to meet someone like me, even if only for a few minutes. It would be very unfair to ask you to tell no one that you've met Jonathan Übermind. However, I think I know a way to guarantee that our research here stays secret."

I imagined Verb and me tied up in sacks and thrown in the back of the panel truck. I started to look around for an escape route.

"Not only can I protect our mission, but I think I can help with your science project as well." Dr. Übermind stopped. We were standing by the front door of the old hotel. "How would you two like the opportunity to join the Übermind Junior Research Institute?"

"Oh, man!" Verb said.

"The what?" I asked.

Verb winced with embarrassment, as if he was ashamed we were related. "Don't you know anything, Theora? There's a whole page about it at the end of all the Übermind Adventures books."

He turned to Dr. Übermind. "See, I told you she doesn't read them."

"The Übermind Junior Research Institute," said Dr. Übermind, "is the best-equipped, most modern, most professionally supervised research facility for young scientists in the world. Did you know that over half the names on *Scientists' Home Journal*'s list of 'Researchers on the Rise' were once members of the Übermind Junior Research Institute? If you can keep quiet about what you saw today, I can arrange for immediate access to the Übermind Junior Research Institute's facilities."

"So it's like a science camp?" I asked.

"I suppose you could call it that."

"We'll have to ask our parents."

D r. Übermind said I could use the phone in his base camp to call them.

We were walking on the gravel drive that led up to the Grand Philodendron Hotel. It was infested with weeds, and we had to kick them out of the way in the places where the truck tires hadn't flattened them.

"If this lake had been in a more remote area, we would have programmed the coordinates into the Übermind Tent Launcher, and our base camp facilities would have been ready and waiting for us when we arrived in the helicopter. In this case, we had to be more subtle."

"That's a shame," said Verb. "The Tent Launcher sounds cool."

We went around the hotel, heading for the private dock on the other side. Passing by the garage, I saw that the truck had PERFECT COVER UPHOLSTERY RESTORERS printed on the side.

"We were lucky to find this abandoned property, which we could buy and use as a very convenient field headquarters. Disguised as upholsterers, we moved in our scientific equipment, and no one suspected a thing."

"This is so neat," said Verb.

We stood at the edge of the dock. Like the hotel, the dock was old and neglected and looked ready to fall apart at any moment. The submarine was tied up on the far end, and the pilot was walking carefully along one of the half-rotten beams back to us. He seemed to be having trouble keeping his balance.

"Let me introduce you to my assistant," Dr. Übermind said as the sub pilot reached dry land. "Theora and Verb Theremin, this is Melvin van Cassowary."

Melvin van Cassowary was tall and very skinny. He looked like he had been made by twisting coat-hanger wires together. He wore thick glasses, and his hair stuck out in all directions.

"Hi." Melvin half waved in an embarrassed way.

Verb peered at Melvin carefully. "What happened to Brick?"

I remembered that name. In the Übermind Adventures books, Dr. Übermind's assistant had been someone named Brick Biggman. He flew Dr. Übermind's planes and tested his inventions and generally helped out. In one of the books I'd read, Brick had fought off an octopus with a plastic fork. I remembered thinking at the time that someone like Brick must be useful to have around.

"Brick doesn't work for the Übermind Institute anymore," Dr. Übermind said, sounding annoyed. "He took another job. Apparently, after his third Komodo dragon bite, Brick decided he would rather teach freshman chemistry at Calpurnia State Teachers' College than expand the frontiers of scientific knowledge."

"You're kidding," Verb said.

"Scientists rarely kid," said Dr. Übermind. "Melvin is a superlative assistant, though. Aren't you, Melvin?"

"Well, yeah, I guess," said Melvin. Ever since Verb had mentioned Dr. Übermind's old assistant, Melvin had looked uncomfortable.

"According to the Übermind Sidekick-o-Matic, the most advanced human-resources computer ever created by man, Melvin was the perfect match for this position. Since an Übermind computer is never wrong, I hired him immediately."

I had never seen Brick Biggman in person, of course, but based on what I had read, Melvin appeared to be the least likely person anyone would pick to replace him. An octopus probably could have taken care of him with a couple of tentacles tied behind its back. I didn't say anything, though. It looked like Melvin had enough problems already without me butting in.

Dr. Übermind fished a set of keys out of his pocket. Attached to the key chain was a small black box that looked like the auto-lock button for my parents' car. He pressed something, and the submarine's lights flashed once, a horn honked, and the hatch swung shut automatically. Slowly the sub sank below the surface of the water until there was nothing visible but the rope that attached it to the dock.

"Unreal," said Verb.

"It's very useful," agreed Dr. Übermind. "Most upholstery restorers don't have a mini-sub. I'd hate to give away our disguise by leaving this one lying around. Shall we go inside?"

Dr. Übermind and Melvin were set up in the basement of the hotel, in a large ballroom with high ceilings and a dingy wooden floor. Half of the room was filled with electronics and chemical equipment.

Verb was impressed. "Come look at these chemicals!" he said to me. "This is way better than what we've got at school."

"Excuse me, where's your phone?" I asked Dr. Übermind. "I really should call home and tell my parents what's happened."

Before he could answer, a siren wailed. Everyone froze.

"Great Scott! It's the distress beacon!" said Dr. Übermind.

"Look!" Melvin pointed to an orange light, the size of an old-fashioned Christmas tree bulb, flashing on one of the control panels.

Dr. Übermind frowned. "It's the priority channel. This is serious business." He frowned some more. "Serious Übermind Business." He took out his key chain and pressed another button. "Kids, I'm afraid we'll have to leave right away. One thing you learn when you're a professional scientist: Don't ignore the orange distress beacon."

Dr. Übermind started stuffing printouts and electronic gadgets into an aluminum suitcase. "Once we're in the air, you can call your parents from the skyphone," he said.

6

Verb was out the door before Dr. Übermind had even finished speaking. I hesitated. Our parents would be furious if we went somewhere with strange people without their permission. On the other hand, I could imagine Dr. Übermind and Melvin forgetting all about us as soon as we got out of their sight. That meant no science project for me and weeks of listening to Verb complaining. If I had to choose between that and upsetting our parents, it wasn't a tough decision.

I picked up my backpack and followed them out. When I got there, Verb was standing on the concrete patio, gawking.

"It's the *Enormous Nellie*," he said in an awestruck voice.

In front of us, floating on the lake, was a huge cargo

plane, painted light blue, with the Übermind Institute logo on the tail. It floated on pontoons, and a long rope ladder hung from a door high up by the cockpit.

"It's a CX-13 cargo plane," Verb said. "It's a prototype. It was built back in 1956, in response to the Danzig Doughnut Crisis."

I stared at him. "Verb, how do you know all this?"

"The *Übermind Technical Manual*," he said. "Duh."

"The *Enormous Nellie* has the largest thrust-to-pastry ratio of any aircraft ever designed," said Dr. Übermind. "She can carry one hundred thousand jelly doughnuts, or fifty thousand éclairs, at full thrust for fourteen hours with negligible losses in fluffiness and filling containment."

"It's a marvel of modern engineering," Melvin said.

"There's only one other CX-13 in existence," said Verb. "That one's being used for top-secret aircraft baking experiments."

"That's correct," said Dr. Übermind. "Even now, researchers at Wright-Patterson Air Force Base are very close to being able to keep a pizza hot and crispy at supersonic speeds."

"How did it get here?"

"It was submerged," Dr. Übermind said, leading us carefully along the dock. "If we didn't want anyone to notice the mini-sub and get suspicious, we certainly didn't want anyone to see the cargo plane."

"But people will see it taking off," I said. "There aren't any seaplanes that land in Lake Philodendron. People are bound to notice."

"Aha," said Dr. Übermind, as we climbed the rope ladder. "There is something different about this plane. Can you spot it?"

I was trying too hard not to fall in the lake to look closely, so I didn't say anything.

"I know," shouted Verb. "It's blue."

"Correct," said Dr. Übermind, helping us aboard. He rolled up the ladder and closed the door, cranking it shut with a metal wheel. "The *Enormous Nellie* has been cleverly camouflaged to look just like the sky. As soon as the plane leaves the water, it will be virtually invisible."

"What about the noise?" I asked.

"If people can't see what made the noise, they won't worry about it," said Dr. Übermind. "Trust me. I have studied human behavior."

"Commencing the preflight checks," Melvin shouted from the cockpit.

"Go ahead," Dr. Übermind replied. "Don't forget to lock the doors to the ballast tanks. We don't want them flying open in midair and scooping up another flock of geese."

"Good point." Melvin flipped a switch, then pressed it a couple of extra times to make sure it was in the right position.

Verb couldn't contain himself any longer. "Look at all

this!" he said. "I'm actually inside the *Enormous Nellie*! I have to call Lloyd Hemlock—he'll never believe it!"

"Verb," I said, "we're only here because we promised we wouldn't tell anybody, remember?"

Verb whimpered a bit. This was the coolest thing that had ever happened to him, and now he couldn't even brag about it. It was giving him fits. I kind of felt bad for the little guy.

"I'll find you the skyphone," said Dr. Übermind. "You should contact your parents as soon as possible."

While he searched the cockpit, I had a chance to look around the cabin. Instead of the usual rows of seats, it had more racks of electronic gear bolted against the walls. There was an enormous map of the world that showed a glowing dot wherever an Übermind Institute team was working. There was a dot by Lake Philodendron, with the words SECRET MISSION in tiny letters beneath it.

"Look! The Briefing Table!" The way Verb said it, I could hear the capital letters. It was a long conference table at the back of the cabin with computer terminals set into each place.

"Which one of these chairs did the President sit in?"

"Which president?" asked Dr. Übermind, handing me the phone.

I could tell that Verb couldn't wait to start running around touching everything.

We heard a sort of growling whine, like the beginning of a Motörhead song, and the whole plane started to vibrate. Through the window, I saw us drifting away from the dock and the Grand Philodendron Hotel.

"Buckle up," said Dr. Übermind. "Here we go."

Melvin was in the pilot's chair, and Dr. Übermind joined him in the cockpit. Verb and I watched through the windows as we picked up speed, then rose above the lake and into the air. As soon as the plane had stopped climbing, Verb jumped out of his chair and ran over to the big TV that was built into the wall.

"Verb, stay in your seat," I said. "The 'fasten seat belt' light is on."

"When you reach your parents on the skyphone, let me speak to them," said Dr. Übermind, turning around in his chair. "Sometimes it helps to have a famous person explain things.

"Feel free to watch a movie while we fly," he said to Verb, who was busy opening the cabinets under the TV screen. "We have *Planet of the Apes, Beneath the Planet of the Apes,*

Escape from the Planet of the Apes, Conquest of the Planet of the Apes, and *Gidget*."

"What about *Battle for the Planet of the Apes*?" I asked.

"It's on the other plane. I'm sorry."

"Ooh, *Gidget*." My brother's eyes got big. "Really?"

"Forget it, Verb," I said.

"Come on, please? Just while you're calling Mom and Dad?" He folded his hands and tried to look sweet, which fools no one, least of all me. *Gidget* is his favorite movie in the world. I would rather eat a bug. Because of Verb, I have had to see *Gidget* more times than I can remember, and if I never hear another song by the Four Preps again, it'll be too soon.

I shrugged at him, pretending not to care. "Go ahead," I said.

I wasn't just being a good sister. I knew from previous experience that it would have ended up as a wrestling match if I'd tried to take the tape out of his hands, and I didn't want to cause a scene. Verb settled in to watch his movie, and I dialed the skyphone.

I won't repeat the conversation I had with my parents. It wasn't easy trying to explain to them who we had met, where we were, and what we were doing. I'll just say that by the time I handed the skyphone over to Dr. Übermind, *Gidget* was half over. I love my parents, but they can be a little thick sometimes.

Dr. Übermind explained that he had been sightseeing in

Philodendron Landing and overheard us arguing about a physics problem. Part of his mission in life was to reward such scientific curiosity, he said, and so he had offered us membership in the Übermind Junior Research Institute.

Verb was still intently watching his movie. I was very relieved. When he's bored and no one is paying attention to him, my brother has a tendency to get out his Swiss Army knife and poke his nose into places he's not supposed to. Here on his hero's super-scientific aircraft, full of locked cabinets and computer files, I had been afraid he would do something to get us booted down to the cargo hold, or even into parachutes and off the plane entirely.

"Hey," Melvin called over his shoulder. "Could you open that mini-fridge by the side of the couch? I could really go for a fig right now."

I tossed him a fig and took some grapes for myself. It looked like Dr. Übermind wouldn't be getting off the skyphone any time soon. After *Gidget* was over, and I had convinced Verb that we didn't need to watch it again, we put in one of the other movies. It wasn't until the ape army had reached the Forbidden Zone in *Beneath the Planet of the Apes* that Dr. Übermind finally hung up.

"I'm sorry," I said.

"Not at all. Your parents are charming people. And thorough. It's rare to find nonscientists as thorough as that. In the end, though, after hearing about the superlative opportunities offered by the Übermind Junior Research Institute, they were thrilled to give their permission. Of course, after we take care of this emergency at Station 47, we'll fly back to Lake Philodendron so they can sign all the necessary permission slips and injury release forms."

"Injury release forms?"

"Don't worry. It's merely a technicality."

Dr. Übermind left Melvin to handle the flying and sat down to watch movies with us. I love the Planet of the Apes movies, but they're a little hard to handle one right after another. Eventually, I sort of zonked out.

When I woke up, Dr. Übermind was back in the co-pilot's seat and the plane's engines were making a different sound. It felt like we were getting ready to land.

I looked out the windows, but all I could see was heavy gray clouds. Eventually, a runway appeared in the mist and we bounced to a stop. The fog was thicker on the ground than it was from the air, and I could only barely see a couple of buildings on the edge of the runway. We sat there for a few seconds, then Doctor Übermind stood up and stretched.

"We've arrived at Station 47," he said. "Welcome to the Pacific Northwest!"

8

"**O**oh, Bigfoot!" said Verb.

Dr. Übermind shook his head. "Sorry, not this trip. We're on the trail of something far more interesting than the common Sasquatch."

Melvin opened the cabin door, and the airport's ground crew, dressed in Übermind Institute blue coveralls, rolled a metal ladder up to the side of the plane. We climbed down, and the crew attached cables to the *Enormous Nellie* and started dragging it into a hangar.

"This is Station 47, the Institute's primary research base for Oregon, Washington, and British Columbia," said Dr. Übermind.

Verb looked around, thrilled. All I could see was a few buildings and fog. I shivered. The fog was turning into rain. I remembered Mom telling me to take my jacket when I left the house after school. I felt a little foolish.

"As soon as we get the gear stowed and the rest of the team assembled, we'll be ready to proceed," said Dr. Übermind. "There's not a moment to lose."

We heard shouting coming from the hangar. The crew

dragging the *Enormous Nellie* had stopped. The cargo plane's wings were wedged against the sides of the door, and it appeared to be stuck.

"Oh, man," said Melvin. He sprinted over to help. I was about to follow him, since I had forgotten my backpack on the plane, when Verb stopped me.

"Look!" He pointed up into the fog. "Do you hear that?"

"What?"

"The engine."

I could hear it now, a high-pitched roar. It got louder, and we saw a dark shape emerge out of the fog. It was another airplane, coming in for a landing.

The plane got closer. The noise of the engines was now all I could hear. I didn't know much about airports, but I wondered if it was safe to be standing here on the runway like this. Verb and Dr. Übermind didn't seem to notice.

Verb shouted in my ear. "It's the ÜB-2!" He pointed. The plane had just touched the tarmac and was now screaming toward us. "The Übermind Industries long-range reconnaissance aircraft."

"Great." I wanted to run, but if Verb wasn't going to, neither was I.

Fishtailing a little, the ÜB-2 skidded to a halt.

The plane was long and black, with a splashy version of the Übermind Institute logo painted on the twin tail fins. It had two sets of wings—stubby triangular ones back by the engine, and a smaller set up by the cockpit.

As we were watching, the glass canopy flipped open, and a flexible metal ladder unrolled to the ground. The pilot took a briefcase from behind his seat, climbed down, and ran over to join us.

"Sorry I'm late," he said, taking off his black, bubble-shaped helmet. "I had a little trouble with a crosswind over the Atlantic."

"Johnny Übermind," Verb said.

He looked like a younger copy of Dr. Übermind, right down to the same perfect hair and pointy chin. He was kind of cute, too. As cute as Dylan McMasterson from school, which is to say, pretty cute. But he had the same crazy look in his eyes as Verb and Dr. Übermind. I took a step back.

"Son, you landed far too close to us," said Dr. Übermind, pointing to where the plane stood. "If I hadn't trusted you completely, I would have had to get out of the way. I have told you a thousand times about observing proper safety procedures while landing. Especially in befogged conditions such as these."

"Gee, sorry, Dad. I guess I was in such a rush to make up time that it slipped my mind."

Dr. Übermind shook his head. "The most important time to follow proper procedures is when?"

"When you don't feel like following them," Johnny recited. I noticed that Verb was mouthing the words along with him. It must have been a well-known saying at the Übermind Institute.

"These are two new members of the Übermind Junior Research Institute," Dr. Übermind said. "They had just agreed to join us when the orange distress beacon went off. This is Verbert Theremin."

Johnny shook Verb's hand. "Pleased to meet you," he said.

"And his sister, Theora."

"Hi," I said.

"Hello," he said, staring at me. "My name's Johnny. Johnny Übermind. It's very nice to meet you."

"Thank you. It's nice to be here," I said.

"Johnny, did you bring the data?" Dr. Übermind asked.

"Sure. It's all in here." He patted the briefcase and smiled at me in a goofy way. I pretended not to notice. "Orbital photos from *UberSky One*, weather reports, and the most recent set of migratory pattern extrapolations."

"What about the nets? Did you bring the new nets?"

"You bet, Dad. The nets are in the cargo hold. They're made from the special composite cord I've been experimenting with, and I adjusted the Übermind Turbo Loom to tie double knots at all the intersections. My tests say they ought to be unbreakable."

Verb raised his hand. "Pardon me," he said. This was the most polite I had ever seen him, including at school and church. "But what are the nets for?"

"I suppose it's time that I told you the facts of the case," Dr. Übermind said. "Even though you may find some of this unbelievable, be assured that it is—"

He stopped, listening intently to something I couldn't hear.

"Duck!"

I heard a buzz that reminded me of an angry bee, felt a rush of air, and then I was on the ground, my head hitting the earth with a thump. Johnny Übermind had tackled me.

"What are you doing?" I asked.

"I'm really sorry," he said. He blushed bright red and sprang back to his feet. "Here, let me help you up.

"This is something that we've been working on in the lab," he continued. "The Very Mobile Phone. It's a telephone you don't have to carry around—if you get a call, it comes looking for you."

Dr. Übermind put the phone to his ear. "Übermind here."

"Wow!" Verb said. "Is that what you were working on during *The Adventure of the Galloping Gargoyle*? The part where you were showing the diplomats around your lab? You said you were doing experiments on telepathic telecommunications devices. Is this it?"

"I'd forgotten that was in the book," said Johnny. "But don't tell anyone, all right? We're still working on it."

Johnny smiled at me again, then nervously looked away. I wondered if I had done something to make him uneasy. I checked my clothes. Nothing looked out of place. I couldn't remember what I'd had for lunch—was there food in my teeth?

Dr. Übermind was nodding into the phone. "Yes? Yes. I see. I understand."

He hung up. "That was the Oregon Commissioner for Sideshow Affairs. She's been detained. We'll have to meet her there."

He shouted at Melvin, who was still struggling with the rest of the Übermind ground crew. "Leave the plane where it is! There's no time! Unpack the Übermind Suitcase Helicopter. We'll fly that to the site of the latest attack."

"Attack?" I asked.

Dr. Übermind looked grim. "Bats."

"Bats?"

"You may have learned in your science classes that bats do not attack humans," Dr. Übermind said. "This is true.

40

However, certain bats can cause serious problems when confronted with their natural enemies."

"Birds?" suggested Verb.

Dr. Übermind shook his head. "Circuses."

"What?" I didn't believe what I'd just heard.

"There is a species of bat, known to scientists as *Vespertilioingens tarpaulinsis*, that is native to the Transylvanian region of Central Europe. It is driven wild by the presence of tarpaulin, the fabric used to make circus tents."

"The tarpaulin bats of Transylvania are responsible for the disappearance of three traveling circuses in Europe in the past six months," said Johnny. "The latest victims, the Flying Helmecki Brothers, vanished for an entire month before Übermind search teams found them in a cave, trapped beneath a heap of guano and chewed-up tarpaulin."

"Eww," I said.

Dr. Übermind nodded. "Eww, indeed. Recently, our researchers at Station 47 have been detecting what appears to be tarpaulin bat activity here in North America. They must have had a new sighting today, which is why they activated the orange distress beacon."

"If the tarpaulin bats have indeed expanded their range to this continent, well, I don't have to tell you what that means," said Johnny. "Unless we can invent a way to deter these animals, soon no big top in the entire world will be safe."

Verb's eyes were huge. Being not only a junior scientist but a pretty weird kid as well, he thought bats were cool.

"How many tarpaulin bats does it take to carry off an entire circus?" he asked in a hushed voice.

Dr. Übermind examined the printouts that Johnny had handed him. "According to our sources, about four or five—"

"Four or five hundred bats?" Verb squeaked, interrupting.

"Four individual bats. Possibly five," said Dr. Übermind.

They had to be joking.

"It's true," Johnny said. "These are no ordinary bats, Theora. You know how the Malayan flying fox is one of the world's biggest bats and has a wingspan of six feet? Well, our biologists estimate that the tarpaulin bats of Transylvania have a wingspan of *sixty*."

"Hang on," I said. "How could a bat fly if it had wings that big? I mean, they wouldn't be able to support themselves, right?" I remembered this from Mr. Pinweed's class. "They'd just collapse under their own weight."

I stopped. "What's that noise?"

Johnny shook his head. "I don't hear anything."

It was a rustling noise from somewhere in the distance. And it was getting closer.

Verb squinted into the fog. "Over there!"

"Get the nets!" shouted Dr. Übermind. Then we all saw it.

A dark shape swooped toward us from out of the sky. It was still far away, but it was clear that the thing, whatever it was, was huge. Two yellow eyes shone as it bore down on us.

"It's in a feeding frenzy!" shouted Dr. Übermind. "Run!"

"Into the hangar! Follow us!" Johnny took off, with his father one step behind. Verb would have gone, too, if I hadn't been holding on to his arm.

"What are you doing?" he squealed, trying to wriggle free. "We have to get out of here!"

I wasn't listening. I was watching the big black bat glide toward us, getting larger by the second.

"Theora!"

I didn't let go. "Verb, wait," I said. "It's not a bat at all."

"Come on! You heard Dr. Übermind!"

"It's not a bat, Verb. It's not flapping its wings. It's not real."

I watched it come closer. "I think it's a kite."

Then it was on us. I felt something grab at my clothes, and there was a smell like a cheap plastic windbreaker. Then I was in the air.

"Hey!" It was Verb's voice, coming from somewhere close. All I could see was black fabric in front of my face. I twisted around and could see the ground, getting farther away by the second.

"I told you so," I said. The kite was all black, and the

"eyes" were two yellow patches sewn onto the material. The bottom half of the kite, where Verb and I were stuck, was covered with strips of duct tape, rolled into circles so that the sticky side faced out.

"Verb, are you all right?"

"No."

"I think we're okay," I said. "The duct tape looks strong. It should hold us."

"You think so?"

I tried to sound brave, which was hard to do hundreds of feet in the air. "Sure," I said.

"Do you really mean that?"

"Maybe."

A thin rope was tied to the kite's frame. I saw it tighten, and the kite bucked against the change of direction.

"Hang on, Verb. I think we're being reeled in."

We had left the Übermind research station far behind and were heading for a nearby town. The kite lost altitude as we got closer. Soon I could see houses and individual people on the street. I shouted and waved at some of them who were out working in their yards, but they didn't even look up. I was annoyed. Not only was I yelling my head off but there was this big huge thing that looked like a bat flying right over their houses. Adults just don't pay attention.

We flew past more houses, heading toward the center of town, getting lower all the time. Soon we would be able to see who was on the other end of the kite string. Ahead of us, I saw a brown-and-orange sign that looked familiar.

"Oh, no," said Verb.

"What?"

"We're heading for Burger Buckaroo."

Verb was right. It was a Burger Buckaroo sign. There was no mistaking the Burger Buckaroo mascot, a hamburger wearing little cowboy chaps, making the thumbs-up gesture. Even from the air, I started to notice the unmistakable smell of Burger Buckaroo grease.

Verb began to struggle again, trying to free himself from the duct tape. My brother has a thing about Burger Buckaroo. Inside each restaurant, they have a big statue of the mascot standing at the entrance. That's scary enough, but there's also a motion sensor or something inside to let it know when people come in. So every time you go to a Burger Buckaroo, this giant hamburger, which is about six feet tall, turns around and says "Howdy!" This freaks Verb out completely. However, he loves their Trail Ride Fries with Laredo Seasoning too much to stop going. I think this combination of fear and desire has done something to his mind.

While Verb thrashed around, I saw a man standing on the roof, reeling in the kite string. He turned the crank again, and the kite jerked forward. We reached the roof, then lost our lift suddenly and fell the last few feet onto the shingles.

Buried under the collapsed kite and still caught in the duct tape, I could hear the man say, "It worked! I don't believe it. I finally got a good one!"

"Little help?" I asked. Verb was making wild-animal noises, trying to get free. I imagined it wouldn't be too long before he wigged out, and I didn't blame him.

"Hang on, hang on," the man said. "I'll get you out in a second. Okay, wait a minute. You're still caught in the tape, right? If you pull slowly now, you should be able to get free. I'll hold the kite up to give you some room."

It took us a few minutes, but we finally got loose.

The man dropped the kite. "I can't believe this at all. I'm so happy you're here," he said.

He was sort of vacant-eyed, with slicked-back hair that stuck up in a couple of places. His blazer had a Burger Buckaroo emblem over the pocket, and his tie was striped with the Burger Buckaroo colors, brown and orange. He had a big happy smile on his face, like he couldn't believe his good luck. On his lapel was a shiny metal name tag that read "Mr. Saa—Your Manager."

He looked at the jumble of struts and fabric and duct

tape. "This capture kite was the best six bucks I ever spent."

He walked over to the ladder that led down to the sidewalk. "You look tired," he said. "You're probably tired. I bet you're tired. Just come this way, if you don't mind, and I'll explain everything. I really will."

Verb and I glanced at each other. Verb looked worried. Usually I like to tease him about his phobia, but now wasn't the right time. I was too worried myself. There was something about this Mr. Saa person that seemed very odd.

Carefully, we climbed down the ladder and followed Mr. Saa into the restaurant. I wasn't sure what other option we had.

"Howdy, folks!" said the Burger Buckaroo mascot as we passed it. "Try our new Super Cowpoke Burger—it's got twice as much lettuce as before! Twice as much!" Then it waved at us, its metal arm swinging stiffly back and forth.

Verb whimpered. I held his hand.

Mr. Saa stopped in his tracks and tapped on the side of the big hamburger. "I thought I told you the new special of the week was the Deep-Fried Cactus Strips."

"Sorry, pardner," said the mascot.

Verb whimpered again. Deep down, I know he's sure that one of these days the Burger Buckaroo mascot is going to step off its little platform and get him.

Mr. Saa went inside, and I followed, dragging Verb along.

Another man in a Burger Buckaroo blazer was working at

47

the counter. He looked a lot like Mr. Saa, and now that I thought about it, they both looked like the guys who ran the Burger Buckaroo in Philodendron Landing.

"Cleevo, look!" said Mr. Saa. "I got one!"

"You got two," said Cleevo, wiping down the counter with a rag.

"I got one and a spare. Even better!"

Mr. Saa led us around the counter and into the back of the restaurant, where there was a small office in one corner. Besides the desk and chair, there were framed photographs of the moon on the walls and a little radio was playing the Muzak version of "Chain Saw." Mr. Saa, in his blazer, stood by the desk, still smiling.

"I can't tell you how terrific this is," he said. He leaned forward to shake our hands. "Please, call me Tsam."

"Tsam?" I repeated.

"The *T* is almost silent, but not quite," he said. "It's a family name."

"Nice to meet you," I said, introducing Verb and myself. His hand was cold. Ice cold.

"Why did you bring us here?" I asked. Even though this guy had a (sort of) Ramones song on his radio, that didn't mean I trusted him.

Tsam smiled some more. "I bet you're hungry. How about a Burger Buckaroo Super Special before we go? Maybe some Unbelievable Shakes? On the house, of course."

"What do you mean 'before we go'?"

"I'd like some Trail Ride Fries," Verb said.

I blocked his way. "Forget it, Verb. We're not hungry."

That wasn't true. I was starving, and the smell of Burger Buckaroo food, drifting in from under the door, wasn't helping any. Something about this Tsam guy just wasn't right, though, and I didn't want to take anything from him.

"Oh, man, I am really getting off on the wrong foot here," Tsam said nervously. "Not just one wrong foot. Two. Two wrong feet. Look, why don't I just be honest?"

"That's a good idea," I said.

"Theora, how would you like to be in a beauty pageant?"

"Excuse me?" This was getting more insane by the second. If I had to, I wondered if I could knock Tsam down long enough for Verb and me to escape out into the street. Probably so, I thought.

Tsam must have understood the wild expression on my face, because he backed away, holding his hands up in front of him. "Okay, wait. Let me change first, and maybe you'll understand things a little bit better. Just stay here for a second. Excuse me." He disappeared into the bathroom at the back of the office.

We'd been kidnapped by a crazy guy with a giant kite, and we were stuck in a fast-food restaurant hundreds of miles from home. I was afraid to find out what was going to happen next.

"Stay close to me," I said to Verb.

"Thanks for waiting." The door to the bathroom swung open. Mr. Tsam Saa, manager of the Burger Buckaroo, was gone. In his place was a giant insect.

"Is this better?" it asked.

I didn't scream, but that didn't mean I wasn't shocked. Even Verb, who keeps all kinds of grotesque things in tanks in his room, took a step back.

"Is it too much?" asked the giant insect. "I knew it would be too much. I knew it. I really did give this a lot of thought, but I just couldn't find an easy way to introduce myself. Encounters between human beings and my people usually don't begin well. I'm sorry if I startled you."

"Startled? You're a bug!" I couldn't stop staring. Here was a six-foot-tall bug, standing on its hind legs and talking to Verb and me as if it were the most normal thing in the world.

"Wow," Verb said, tugging on my sleeve. "Do you know what he is?"

"A bug!"

"Really, I can explain everything," said Tsam.

"There was a whole chapter in the *Übermind Encyclopedia of Mysterious Creatures* about this. Theora, this is a South American Giant Whining Cockroach!"

Tsam the insect inclined his big triangular head to one side. "Not exactly," he said. "The large, noise-making cockroaches of Earth are our cousins. We use them to help keep our Burger Buckaroo restaurants free of other insect pests. That's why you'll never see a bug in a Burger Buckaroo."

"Until now," said Verb.

"Why are you still wearing a tie?" I asked. I know it wasn't a very intelligent question, but I think I was in some kind of shock.

"It's a hyperdimensional tie," said Tsam, wiggling the tie with one of his four free legs. "It's what allows us to disguise ourselves as humans. The Burger Buckaroo Corporation buys them in bulk from Abercrombie & Klaarg."

The full meaning of what Tsam had said earlier finally reached me. "Are you saying that everyone who works at a Burger Buckaroo is actually . . ."

"A giant cockroach from the moon," said Tsam. "Yep, that's pretty much it."

"The moon?"

"Well, we don't *call* it the moon, but yeah, that's where we're from."

"What do you call it?" Verb asked.

"Bob."

"Really?"

"You probably haven't heard of it, have you?" asked Tsam.

"We've heard of the moon," I said. "But I don't think anybody's heard that the moon is inhabited by giant cockroaches who call it Bob."

"This will be a scientific breakthrough," said Verb, sounding just like Dr. Übermind.

"So it's probably a good bet that you haven't heard of *Thrilling Cockroach Tales* magazine, have you?" Tsam asked. "That's where I got the kite. They always advertise something cool on the back page. Anyway, the magazine's kind of the reason why you're here."

It was hard to follow what Tsam was saying. I kept getting distracted by the way his antennae bobbed when he talked. I had never seen an insect's head in such detail before, except on TV nature shows, and that wasn't really the same thing. I kept thinking that I ought to be terrified, but the truth was, Tsam was a lot less creepy as a bug than he had been as a person. He made more sense this way.

Tsam opened one of the desk drawers and pulled out a magazine. On the cover it had a picture of a Moon Cockroach wearing a crown and a pink sash. The Moon Cockroach was holding a bouquet of roses.

There were strange squiggly symbols that looked like words, but I didn't know what language they were in.

"Oh, hold on a second," said Tsam, grabbing a spray can from the drawer. Before I knew what was happening, he had sprayed both of us with it.

"Language spray," he explained. "Moon Cockroachese is very difficult to master, so we developed this to help out visitors. It wears off in a couple of days."

He handed the magazine back to me. My eyes were watering and everything smelled like lemon furniture polish, but I could read the Moon Cockroachese writing as well as I could read English.

BEAUTY QUEEN SECRETS REVEALED!
THE EXCITING TRUE STORY OF
HORTENSE BENWAY! (see page 65)

"Wow," said Verb. "Do you have any more of that spray?"

"Forget it," I said. Verb was taking beginning German in school, and I knew what he was thinking.

"Hortense Benway is the most beautiful female in all of Bob," Tsam said. "She was last year's Princess of Neptune, and now she's gone on to become a famous singer throughout the civilized universe. This issue of *Thrilling Cockroach Tales* has the first interview she gave after she won."

Verb and I stared at him. We had no idea what he was talking about.

"Hortense Benway is the most famous Moon Cockroach

ever," he explained. "People can't get enough of her. *Thrilling Cockroach Tales* will print any article they can get that's even remotely about her. So I had this terrific idea. Since the Cavalcade of Loveliness was coming up again—"

"What's that?" I asked. I had too many questions to wait until Tsam stopped talking.

"It's a beauty pageant. It's where they crown the Princess of Neptune."

"Princess of Neptune?"

Tsam sighed. "The winner of the Cavalcade of Loveliness is called the Princess of Neptune. In the old days, when Neptune used to be ruled by whoever was the prettiest, the Princess of Neptune had real power. Now it's just a ceremonial title."

"And this is on Neptune? The planet Neptune?"

"Correct. But it's open to entrants from everywhere," continued Tsam. "So anyway, since the Cavalcade of Loveliness is coming up, I got this great idea. I bet people are dying to know what it's like to be a Cavalcade of Loveliness contestant, just like Hortense Benway."

I started to see what he was going for. "Do you seriously want me to enter this beauty pageant thing so you can write a magazine article about it?"

"Yeah, isn't that great?" said Tsam. He used the exact same tone of voice as my mom when she'd tried to get me to take piano lessons instead of drums.

"Don't worry about the article," he said. "You won't have to write it. All you have to do is go and be a contestant. I'll follow you around and get all the behind-the-scenes information, and I'll write a piece that *Thrilling Cockroach Tales* won't be able to resist.

"What do you say?" Tsam looked at me with a hopeful expression. At least, I think that's what it was. Up until then, I hadn't had any practice reading the faces of giant bugs.

"I don't know about this," I said.

"What does she get if she wins?" asked Verb.

"What *doesn't* she get if she wins?" said Tsam. "If Theora is crowned Princess of Neptune, she receives not only the respect and admiration of her fellow contestants but also valuable scholarships and a truckload of fabulous prizes."

"That sounds good," said Verb.

I held up a hand. "Just a second."

"Oh, come on, please?" asked Tsam. "Please please please? I've been grabbing people all week with my kite, and you're the first one I found who could actually compete in the pageant."

"How many people have you caught?" asked Verb.

"About a dozen. None of them looked right, so I hypnotized them with my tie and sent them on their way."

"It has hypnosis powers, too? That's a heck of a tie."

"Tell me about it. That's how we took care of Neil Armstrong back in 1969."

"And Theora's really the best-looking one?"

"Don't you think so?"

"Excuse me, but there are a few things that I want to know," I said. "First of all, how would we even get to Neptune?"

"Aha," said Tsam. "Transport is no problem. Let me show you."

He pressed a button on his desk. There was a grinding sound, but nothing else happened.

Tsam hissed and switched on the intercom. "Cleevo, the false wall is jammed again. Could you send Priscilla over here, please?"

There was a pause, then Cleevo replied, "Are you sure you want to do this?"

"Look, who's the manager? Just send Priscilla."

Cleevo sighed. "Okay."

In the distance we heard a clanging noise, like someone banging two heavy metal pots together. It got louder and louder with each clang, until it was right outside the office. The door flew open.

It was a huge metal hamburger in a cowboy hat and chaps. It was the Burger Buckaroo mascot.

"Reporting for duty," it said.

Verb yelped and tried to hide behind me.

Tsam pointed to the back wall of the office. "Priscilla, the false wall has malfunctioned. Please take care of it for me."

Priscilla walked stiffly into the office, its metal legs clanging with each step. It stopped by the wall, leaned over, and lifted.

Part of the wall slid up to reveal another door. It was made of clear plastic, and behind it a dark purple light was glowing.

"Check it out," Tsam said. "An interdimensional gateway. A shortcut through time and space. Every Burger Buckaroo franchise has one. We can go from here to Neptune in microseconds."

The robot stepped back and turned stiffly to face Tsam. "Please note that it has been 752 days since this unit's last scheduled maintenance," it said. "If this unit is still under warranty, please contact a big robotic burger-man repair technician at your earliest convenience."

"Thank you, Priscilla. We'll get to it as soon as we can." Tsam patted the top of the robot cowboy hamburger's head. It made a hollow *bong* sound, and Priscilla slowly stomped out of the office.

Tsam watched the robot disappear. "Sometimes I think those things are more trouble than they're worth. We might have been better off when we watched the restaurants by keeping larvae hidden in the salad bars."

Right then I promised myself that I would never eat at a Burger Buckaroo, or for that matter a salad bar, ever again.

Tsam turned back to us. "So you're all set?"

"I've got some more questions," I said. "What about the Überminds?"

Tsam tilted his head to one side. "The who?"

"We were kind of on a field trip." Verb, still sweating from his encounter with Priscilla, explained about the Übermind Junior Research Institute and the tarpaulin bats.

"Well, no problem there," said Tsam. "It sounds like your friends have mistaken my capture kite for one of their tarpaulin bat thingies. They'll probably spend weeks trying to find it. You'll be back in loads of time. It's a short pageant."

"I haven't said I'd do it yet," I said.

I had seen the annual beauty pageant at the Phil Phestival, and it did not look like my idea of a good time. I was sure that Mo Tucker from the Velvet Underground would never be in a beauty pageant. Neither would John Bonham, for that matter. From my point of view, it was about the least cool thing you could do, and I couldn't imagine it would be much different on another planet, no matter what a giant bug in an ugly tie might say.

"Did I mention the fabulous prizes?" Tsam asked weakly.

I had never seen a cockroach look pathetic before. It wasn't very pretty, but it worked.

"All right, look. If I do this, and you can write your article, will you be my science project?" Now that we had gotten separated from the Übermind guys, I needed to come up with something on my own for Mr. Pinweed. Mr. Pinweed would probably turn up his nose at a talking bug from outer space, but at least it was something.

Tsam looked guilty. He rubbed his arms together and adjusted the plates on his shell. "You know, I was planning to just hypnotize you with my tie when this was all over." He paused. "I guess we could work something out."

"All right," I said. "Let's go."

"Yes!" Tsam pumped his four free legs in the air and scuttled over to the controls for his interdimensional gateway thing.

"This is great," Verb said. I think he was most excited about not having to go out past the robot hamburger again. "We'll be the first human beings on Neptune. We need to take careful notes. Boy, I wish I'd brought my camera."

"You don't have a camera."

"Yours, I mean."

"Should we try to send a message to Dr. Übermind?" I asked Verb. "I hate to think of them worrying about where we are, or having to explain to Mom and Dad how they lost us."

"Übermind Institute article seven," he quoted. " 'A little discomfort for science is not a bad thing.' Imagine how proud they'll be when we come back with evidence of creatures from other planets. Dr. Übermind will understand."

The interdimensional gateway made a *ding* sound, like an elevator, and its light turned pink. The clear door slid open.

"Just step through," said Tsam. "Easy as a Burger Buckaroo Hot Apple Pie."

Verb and I went through. There was a flash of color and a weird whistling sound, and all of a sudden we were in a different place.

The first thing I noticed was that we were outside, and the sky was green. We were in a kind of square or big courtyard surrounded by tall buildings. Hung across two of the buildings was a banner that read, WELCOME CAVALCADE OF LOVELINESS CONTESTANTS!

All around us, the square was full of strange creatures rushing in different directions. Most of the creatures were bright green, with big round eyes and stubby noses. They wore metallic silver jumpsuits with black trim and silver helmets that came to a point at the top. A few of them noticed us, but they didn't pay much attention.

These aliens, who I assumed were the Neptunians, were a little shorter than Verb, and it was easy to see over their heads and across the courtyard, where two Moon Cockroaches were waving at us.

"Oh, no," said Tsam, putting his head in his forelegs. "My cousins."

The two giant bugs ran to meet us, dancing around the Neptunians.

"Dude, you found one," said the first Moon Cockroach. It had a "Hello, my name is . . ." sticker on its thorax, with "Delaney" written on it in marker.

"And she's cute, too," said the other, whose sticker read "Harmonic Convergence." It patted Verb on the head. "This one looks like Princess of Neptune material for sure."

Tsam hissed. "The other one, the other one." He pointed to me. "That's the contestant. This one's the brother."

"Oh, sorry, man," said Delaney. "Our mistake."

"Well, you're nice, too," said Harmonic Convergence, looking at me. "I'm sure you'll do just fine."

"Hey, what a coincidence running into you," said Delaney.

He was lying. I could tell. This was the same kind of coincidence that happens when I find my snare drum in Verb's room.

"Since we're here, though," he continued, "I was wondering if you could do us a little favor."

"Such as?" said Tsam.

"Well, you know that Hortense Benway is here, right?"

"Of course she is. She has to crown the new Princess of Neptune, and she's singing a song as part of the between-rounds entertainment."

"So is there, like, any chance you can introduce us to Hortense Benway? I mean, now that we're all part of the pageant and everything."

"*You* are not part of the pageant," Tsam said. "If I had anything to do about it, you wouldn't even be part of the family. You're troublemakers, and I wouldn't introduce you to Hortense Benway even if I knew her, which I don't."

"Dude!" said Delaney, sounding hurt.

"I am here to write a serious journalistic article about life in a beauty pageant for *Thrilling Cockroach Tales* magazine, and you two goofballs are not going to get in the way."

"So you don't know Hortense Benway at all?" asked Harmonic Convergence. "We came out here for nothing?"

"Look, if you want to help, why don't you show Theora's brother the sights of Neptune while we get registered for the Cavalcade of Loveliness," said Tsam.

Verb hates babysitters, and I expected him to run screaming in the other direction, but he didn't. He probably suspected that two giant bugs were going to be more interesting than Jenny Wolf, who usually watches him.

The cousins looked uncertain. If I could have, I would have traded places with them. Seeing the sights of Neptune sounded more fun than being dragged over to this beauty pageant, but I had agreed to do it, and there didn't seem to be any way to get out of it.

Tsam shook his head. "If you two look after Verb, I'll try to get Hortense Benway's autograph if we see her. How's that?"

Harmonic Convergence crouched down until his face was level with Verb's. "Hey, do you want to see the biggest ball of string on Neptune?"

"How big is it?"

Delaney flung four of his legs out wide. "Big."

"Cool," Verb said.

"Meet us in front of the Hall of Contestants after the first round," Tsam called to his cousins, who were already leading Verb away through the crowd of Neptunians.

"Yeah, yeah," said Harmonic Convergence, waving at us before they disappeared.

"Is Verb going to be all right?" I asked.

"Sure. They work at a school for gifted larvae, although you wouldn't know it to look at them."

"Excuse me," said a voice behind us.

It was a Neptunian. "Yes, you. The medium-sized insect and the—what are you exactly, a monkey? Oh, you're not a monkey, are you? You're a human being. I'm so sorry. I make that mistake all the time." There were a number of metal rings hovering over the point of her helmet, and she carried a clipboard.

"My name is Theora," I said. I was more concerned that she had called Tsam "medium-sized" than that she had called me a monkey. If there were insects bigger than Tsam, I really did not want to see them.

"Theora is a lovely name. I'm Eleven Evelyn, and I'm one of the contestant wranglers for the Cavalcade of Loveliness." She raised her clipboard. "Now, which of you is entering the pageant? What am I saying? Of course, you're the contestant, aren't you?" Eleven Evelyn pointed her pen at me.

That was a step in the right direction, I thought. If, right after Tsam's cousins had thought Verb was better-looking than I was, this Neptunian had said the same thing about Tsam, I would have been upset.

"And you are?" she asked, turning to Tsam. "Personal fitness coach? Poise coordinator? Smile technician?"

"Journalist. I'm going to write the story of Theora's experiences for a major intergalactic magazine."

"Well, that's lovely." I don't think she meant it. It was the same tone of voice my mother uses when she hears us practicing in the garage.

Eleven Evelyn made another note on her clipboard. "Well, if you'll please follow me, I'll show you to the Hall of Contestants."

She took off at a quick pace. Tsam and I had to jog to keep up. If it hadn't been for the rings floating over her helmet, we would have lost her in the crowd before we left the square.

We stopped several blocks later in front of a tall silver building with massive columns along its face. Two fountains sprayed water on either side of the steps. The words HALL OF CONTESTANTS—WHERE NEARLY EVERYONE IS BEAUTIFUL were written over the door in big gold letters.

"This way," Eleven Evelyn said, leading us inside.

If I had thought that the Neptunians, in their silver suits and helmets, looked strange, it was nothing compared to what was inside. There were hundreds of different kinds of creatures, all standing in long, orderly lines. Before I had time to study them, Eleven Evelyn had guided us to the end of a line, where we stood behind a pumpkin as big as my parents' Mercury Villager.

The pumpkin rolled around to take a look at us. It had six eyes, with lots of blue eye shadow on all of them.

"This is so exciting," the pumpkin said.

I nodded. "Yeah."

"The Cavalcade of Loveliness has over seven thousand entrants again this year," said Eleven Evelyn. "So, naturally, the first round won't be televised. If we did, our computers tell us that it would take four and a half years. Even for a beauty pageant, that's a little long."

Another Neptunian passed us, carrying a stack of yellow envelopes. Eleven Evelyn took one and opened it up. "Now let's get your entry form filled out so that the MC5000 can process you."

Eleven Evelyn unfolded the form and attached it to her clipboard. "Species?" she asked.

"*Homo sapiens.*" This was something else I remembered from Mr. Pinweed's class. For a class I never liked, it had turned out to be pretty useful. "Common name, human."

"Do you have a family member with you who will look overjoyed if you win and supportive if you lose? It's for the TV robots, so they know where to look."

Tsam raised an arm. "Present."

It was just as well, I thought. I hated to think of what Verb would do if they put him on television.

"I thought you were a journalist," said Eleven Evelyn.

"He's my uncle, too," I said.

"Whatever you say."

Two pink squishy things with dozens of legs crawled by and gave us a look like they didn't believe me, either.

"Planet?" the Neptunian asked.

"Earth."

"Talent?"

"What?"

"What talent will you be demonstrating?" Eleven Evelyn asked. "You know, what are you good at? Ballet? Heavy lifting?"

"I'm a drummer."

Eleven Evelyn winced. "Sorry," she said. "There's a no-drummers rule for this year's contest."

"You've got to be kidding me." Just my luck, I thought, the one thing I could really do well, and there was a rule against it.

"A couple of years ago, the Vleeminoids from Ingspo Minor brought Gina Schock. Then the guys from Andromeda showed up with Samantha Maloney, and somebody else even tried to enter Bob Mould's drum machine. Frankly, it was getting out of hand."

"What else can you do?" Tsam asked. "I mean, you look talented. There's got to be something."

I thought frantically for a second, trying to remember

what I had been doing before the Überminds and Tsam had come into my life.

"I can search for monsters," I said, and regretted it immediately. It wasn't much of a talent. Pretty much anyone could sit on the edge of the lake and look for Big Phil.

Eleven Evelyn was already writing it down. "That's brilliant! That's the neatest talent I've heard since I started working here. You hunt monsters!

"Hey," she said, "maybe you'll get the Beast of the Mall!"

"The what?" I asked, suddenly concerned.

Eleven Evelyn pointed. "There's the MC5000!"

We could finally see to the front of the line. We were all waiting to meet a big white box, about the size of a refrigerator, with wheels at the base and a row of blinking lights along the top.

"The MC5000 is the master of ceremonies and chief data processor for this year's Cavalcade of Loveliness," said Eleven Evelyn. "We're very lucky to have gotten him. The MC5000 won both the 'best buy' and 'best personality (relatively speaking)' awards at last year's robot trade show."

"A real MC5000," said Tsam, in the kind of voice Verb uses to talk about a new Übermind Adventures book. "Does it have the optional sincerity upgrade?"

"You bet. And advanced computational abilities, too. It will process Theora's entry form and decide what her first-round task will be."

"Do you mind if we change that 'I hunt monsters' thing?" I asked, reaching for Eleven Evelyn's clipboard.

She took a step back. "Sorry, it's in ink. Besides, your first idea is always the right one."

"My first idea was 'I'm a drummer.' "

"Are all Earth creatures as nervous as you?"

Up ahead, the MC5000 had extended a claw arm and taken a form from another contestant wrangler, who was pulling a red wagon with a motionless mound of blue fur in it.

"I didn't know *they* would be here," Tsam whispered to me. "Planet Erb hasn't entered a contestant in years, but everyone says they're tough to beat."

"How?" I still hadn't seen the mound of fur move.

"They clean up in the talent rounds. Think about it. When you normally just sit on a rock for two hundred years at a time, anything else you can do is a pretty big step up."

The line moved slowly forward. Each contestant handed her form to the MC5000. The robot fed it into a slot, then its lights flashed and it printed out something, which it handed to the contestant.

"The MC5000 makes sure each first-round task is equally difficult so that everyone gets a fair chance," said Eleven Evelyn. "It would hardly be fair if one person had to compete in the sewage luge, and someone else got competitive napping on Neptune's comfiest easy chair. Honestly, who likes naps?"

All I heard was "sewage luge." "Just what kinds of tasks are these?" I asked.

Eleven Evelyn grinned. "Oh, nothing too terrible. Just some healthy competition designed to challenge the contestants' mental, physical, and aesthetic abilities.

"It's all rigorously supervised," she said, pointing to herself. "We contestant wranglers have never had anyone seriously hurt during the Cavalcade of Loveliness, and we intend to keep it that way."

The rest of the line shuffled forward. I stood still.

"Oh, come on, don't get cold feet now," said Tsam. "Think of my article. Think of your science project."

"Mr. Pinweed won't believe me. If he doesn't believe in Big Phil, he'll give this an F before he gets through with the first paragraph."

"You know, maybe I was overstating," said Eleven Evelyn. We were holding up the line, and she was starting to sound a little anxious. "It's not that dangerous. Doesn't the fact that no one's ever gotten hurt tell you that it's not dangerous?"

"This is a beauty pageant," I said. "Why is there even a *chance* of someone getting hurt? Besides, you didn't say no one's ever gotten hurt. You said no one's ever gotten *seriously* hurt."

"Same difference."

"Not to me."

"Come on, listen to the other assignments," Eleven Evelyn begged. "It's not so bad."

We were now close enough to hear what the MC5000 was saying as it took the contestants' forms.

"The fifth planet of Deneb," it said, processing the form it had received from a quivering, transparent blob. "I visited the fifth planet of Deneb once, many years ago. You were probably still in a test tube back then." The MC5000 laughed, rocking on its thick rubber wheels.

"Beautiful place, the fifth planet of Deneb. Just beautiful. Such friendly folks, too. Everyone says, if you want to see real, down-home Space Jellyfish hospitality, go to the fifth planet of Deneb." Its lights blinked. "Well, according to your entry form, you're a trained opera singer and the best checkers player in your solar system. Not to mention all the volunteer work you've done at the Greater Magellanic Cloud Retirement Home."

The Space Jellyfish quivered with pride. At least, I think it was pride.

A printout emerged from the MC5000's head. "Here we are. Your first-round challenge is—" The robot tore off the printout and read it. "Mrs. Nesbit Sixty-two Gwendolyn, 503B Blastopore Drive. You'll be dusting her collection of antique spoons. Good luck!"

The MC5000 printed out some additional information and handed it to Miss Fifth Planet of Deneb, who slithered away. We all moved forward one place in line, and the next contestant, who looked like the thing on the covers of all the Iron Maiden albums, gave her form to the robot.

I listened closely to the MC5000 when it handed out the next assignment. This wasn't what I had been expecting.

"Mr. Forty-seven Wayne. The last house on the end of Suspicious Row. Shampoo his rugs! Good luck!"

I looked down at Eleven Evelyn. "What's going on?"

"I don't know what you mean."

"This," I said, pointing to the MC5000. "These assignments. This isn't a beauty pageant, this is housework."

"No, it's not. It's a beauty pageant." She held up my entry form and pointed to the title. " 'Cavalcade of Loveliness.' See?"

"Dusting spoons? Shampooing rugs?"

"It's the initial talent round," insisted Eleven Evelyn. "It's to see how well you can, um, clean things, or fix stuff. It's very important to your overall Poise and Good Behavior scores."

Tsam nudged me. "This doesn't sound dangerous at all. I knew you wouldn't have anything to worry about."

"That's not the point," I said. "This is a swindle. You've brought all these people here to be your servants."

"No, really, I swear."

I frowned at Eleven Evelyn and shook my head. I have a pretty good sense of when people are attempting to pawn work off on me. Every week, Verb tries a new scheme to get me to take out the trash for him, and it's given me a lot of practice.

"Stupid perceptive Earth creature," she grumbled. "If I tell you the truth, will you promise not to spread it around?"

"You bet," said Tsam. "You can trust us. We're trustworthy. Go ahead."

"The Cavalcade of Loveliness is a big deal here on Neptune."

"I noticed," I said.

"Almost everybody works on it in some way or other. For me, it's kind of like the family business. My great-great-grandfather, XXVI Gary, founded the pageant, when we first decided that it was a bad idea to make the prettiest person the boss all the time. All my brothers and sisters work for it, too."

"How many is that?" asked Tsam.

"In our clutch of eggs, we had nineteen Evelyns and sixty-two Roys."

"I can barely deal with two cousins," Tsam said. "I can't imagine seventy-five siblings."

"Eighty," I corrected, but I knew what he meant.

"As the pageant got bigger and more people were involved with it, we made a discovery."

"I see where this is going!" Tsam said. "You were so busy with getting ready for the pageant every year that you didn't have time for other jobs, like cleaning your houses."

"Or fixing our flying cars, or trimming our atomic shrubs."

Tsam waved his antennae with excitement. "So you added a new round to the pageant. A round of chores. Brilliant!"

"Kind of," I said.

"Don't hate us because we're practical."

"Your form, please," said the MC5000. We had reached the head of the line.

Tsam rubbed his legs together, making a noise like a cricket. "Here we go!"

The robot started processing my paper. "It's been a while since we've had anyone from Earth," it said. "So nice to have you back again. I hope you'll enjoy your stay here."

"Thank you."

"Ooh, *monster hunting*!" The MC5000 must have just gotten to that part of the entry. "I have the perfect assignment for you. You're just going to love it."

A pink ribbon slid out of a slot on the side of the robot. Eleven Evelyn tore off the end and made a loop out of it.

"Here's your sash," she said.

It was one of those stupid sashes that everyone wears in beauty pageants. It had the words MISS EARTH printed on it. Feeling dumb, I slipped it over one shoulder.

The MC5000 flashed its lights again. "Congratulations, Miss Theremin. You're officially entered in our pageant. I hope nothing bad happens to you."

The robot handed me its printout. "You're off to the Neptune Galleria. Your assignment—capture the Beast of the Mall! Good luck!"

"How come they got spoons and carpet shampooing and I got a beast?" I demanded. We were walking down the hall toward the teleporter booths, following a plum-colored lobster creature whose sash read MISS SQUEVESH. Eleven Evelyn was on my left, Tsam on my right, and I was arguing with both of them.

"It's really a compliment," said Eleven Evelyn. "The assignments are all electronically balanced by the MC5000, re-member? He must have thought you could handle it."

"Great."

"See, you were worried that you'd have to do something boring," said Tsam. "Doesn't this sound exciting? Beasts! Malls! Stuff like that! Isn't that better than, say, vacuuming or something?"

When we found a free teleporter, the three of us got in and Eleven Evelyn dialed in the location of where we were supposed to go. In a flash, we were standing in a parking lot.

I heard a thump. Next to me, Tsam had fallen over. He was lying on his back, wiggling his legs in the air. I helped him up.

"Sorry about that," he said. "Neptunian teleporters always make me a little dizzy."

Eleven Evelyn flipped open a metal compact and checked to make sure that her helmet was still straight.

"Here we are," she said, putting the compact away. "The Neptune Galleria."

Ahead of us, across the parking lot, was a huge, sprawling building. All I can say about it is that, even though I was on another planet, I knew it was a mall. It had tall windows and was decorated with green and yellow trim. I saw dozens of glass-canopied entrances.

"Are you impressed?" asked Eleven Evelyn.

Tsam nodded. "I am. It's big and shiny."

"I was a mall studies major in college, so I know all about the Neptune Galleria," Eleven Evelyn said. "Years ago, our ancestors, who were convinced that they were the smartest people who ever hatched, decided that we needed something to set ourselves apart from other planets. So they discussed and discussed, and after the longest meeting in the history of Neptune, they built this. They built the greatest mall anyone had ever seen."

"Where is everybody?" I asked, scanning the empty parking lot. "At home, the malls are usually packed. Is everyone working on the pageant?"

"Well, kind of," Eleven Evelyn said. "I mean to say, yes, they are working on the pageant, but they wouldn't have been here anyway." She glanced uncomfortably at me. "This is where the Beast of the Mall comes in."

"I see."

"Our ancestors had built the Neptune Galleria too well. It was too big, too shiny, too comfortable. Their attempt to create perfection brought doom upon themselves. No sooner was the great Galleria built than the green skies of Neptune began to darken."

Eleven Evelyn paused. "Are you sure you haven't heard this before? After all, this is from the *Malliad*, the official epic poem of Neptune."

Tsam shrugged four of his legs helplessly. "Sorry."

"Never heard of it," I said. "In fact, I didn't even know that anyone lived on Neptune. I thought all the big planets in the solar system were just huge balls of gas with no real solid part. We even sent space probes past Neptune. Why didn't we ever see you?"

Eleven Evelyn squinted at me. "You know, I don't mean to be critical, but I don't see how a planet can send out one dinky little half-broken space probe and think it knows all there is to know about everything."

"That's a good point."

"What happened with the mall?" Tsam asked.

"An invasion fleet. The Poison Squid Creatures, drawn by our brightly colored grand-opening flyers, arrived from Pluto, determined to take the mall for themselves."

"Wow," said Tsam.

"But in a heroic struggle that lasted an entire day and a half, the Neptune Safety Patrol drove them away, out of the mall and back to the cold depths of space from whence they came."

"A day and a half?" Tsam didn't sound impressed.

"You bet. The story of the battle takes up seventeen chapters in the *Malliad*. But that's not the worst of it. Before the Poison Squid Creatures flew away in their ugly green squid-ships, they cursed us."

"With profanity?" asked Tsam.

"Worse. They decided that if they couldn't have the mall, then no one would."

"But there it is, right there. You've got it."

"But no one can go in."

"Why not?"

"Because of the Beast!" Eleven Evelyn said. "Before they left, the Poison Squid Creatures released a hideous Beast into the mall as their final act of revenge."

Tsam looked at me. "This is going to make such a great article. Have I mentioned how much I appreciate this?"

I didn't say anything.

"When our names are on the cover of *Thrilling Cockroach Tales*, we'll all have a big laugh about this."

"Or," said Eleven Evelyn, "you will receive the finest care that our sponsor, Neptune Discount Hospitals, can provide. Either way, kind of cool, huh?"

Just then, the floating rings on Eleven Evelyn's helmet made a strange hooting noise, which made me think of all the *Planet of the Apes* movies I'd watched on the Übermind plane.

"That's the starting horn," said Eleven Evelyn. "You'd better get going. They add points for speed, you know."

"All right," said Tsam, patting me on the shoulder, "I have a lot of faith in you, so get out there and do your best. Be sure to take notes, too. This is probably going to be the main part of my article." He shoved me forward.

"Just a second," I said. "Do I need some equipment or anything? Am I going to be okay the way I am?"

"You're perfect the way you are, Theora," said Tsam. "Don't change a thing. Now go get 'em!"

Eleven Evelyn appeared concerned. "You mean you don't have any equipment?"

"Do you *see* any equipment?" I'm usually not very sarcastic, except sometimes to Verb, but I was under a lot of stress, and I thought that was the dumbest question I had heard all day.

"I thought you might have had a Microscopic Force Field Projector or a Paralo-Ray Belt Buckle or something. A lot of people do, you know." She sounded hurt.

"I'm sorry," I said. "I didn't mean it. I'm just a little worried."

Eleven Evelyn turned to Tsam. "You didn't bring anything for her?"

"How was I supposed to know?" He gave me another nudge with one of his legs. "Get going. You're on the clock."

Eleven Evelyn looked at the massive, empty mall across the parking lot, then back at us. "Maybe you're right," she said. "Tell you what, you go ahead, and I'll catch up when I've found some equipment for you to use."

"Really?"

"I'm a contestant wrangler. That's my job."

Thanking Eleven Evelyn and hoping that she could find me before whatever lived in the mall did, I jogged to the closest entrance.

"Good luck!" called Tsam, waving goodbye.

Inside the Neptune Galleria, it was completely quiet. The only light came from the red exit signs that hung from the ceiling. It looked like a pretty nice mall, but without the lights, and without the normal noises of air-conditioning and background music, it was spooky. It would have been spooky even without a monster hiding in the shadows some-where.

I was surprised to notice that I was thinking about Verb. I hoped he was all right with Tsam's cousins. Verb being Verb, I imagined that wandering around on another planet in the company of two giant bugs from the moon would probably make his year. Still, I was concerned.

I decided to start at the top and work down, searching each floor. As I walked up the immobile escalators, the quiet began to get to me. It felt like I was the only person in the en-tire world. Usually when that happens, it helps to get out my sticks and play a little, just to make noise and take my mind off things. My sticks, though, were in my backpack, which was right now in the Übermind plane, which was a long way away.

I tapped out parts of "Sheer Heart Attack" on the escalator rail with my hands, but it didn't make me feel any better. The beats faded into the darkness without any echo.

By the time I reached the sixth floor, I was listening hard. That's what happens when you're someplace completely quiet—you get preoccupied by listening for some sound, any sound, to break the silence.

I was listening so hard that when Eleven Evelyn said "Hello, Theora," it sounded like she was using a bullhorn.

"Wow," Eleven Evelyn said. "You really jumped! That was like three feet or something. You ought to play basketball. You're going to be spectacular in the laser gymnastics round."

I had never been so shocked in my entire life. Not even when Verb got into my room and rigged up my door so a big plastic spider fell on my head when I opened it. Now, unlike that time, I wouldn't even have the satisfaction of beating up the person who had shocked me.

"How did you get up here?" I asked, after a minute or two had passed and I could speak again.

"I climbed the fire escape. The Beast never goes outside, so that's safe."

"How did you know where I was?"

"Every contestant wrangler has a special psychic link with her contestant. It's a whole lot easier that way than fooling around with schedules and things."

Eleven Evelyn opened the black plastic trash bag she was carrying. "I managed to find some equipment," she said. "I didn't want to spend too much time looking, because I was worried that the Beast might eat you."

She stopped, glancing at me. "Did I say *eat*? I meant *find*."

"Thanks."

She handed me something from the bag. "This is a PS-5."

"It looks like a stick."

"It's a PS-5."

"It's a stick," I said. "Someone's carved one end into a point. This is a pointy stick."

"No it isn't. Pointy sticks are low-tech and boring. This is a PS-5. The latest model."

I was about to say that just because it was the latest model, that didn't make it not a stick, when Eleven Evelyn handed me something else.

"And here we have a defensive shield. Lightweight. One-handed operation. Easy to use. An excellent complement to the PS-5."

The defensive shield looked a lot like an old aluminum garbage can lid, the kind with the handle welded onto the top.

"I see," I said.

"This is the top of the line," said Eleven Evelyn. "Well, pretty much. I mean, I was trying to find something as fast as I could, and this was the best I could do. I hope you think it's all right."

Eleven Evelyn looked so apologetic that I had to say something nice. "It's great," I lied. "No, really it is. I'm sure it'll be fine."

To myself, I was promising not to get anywhere near the Beast, whatever it was, while I was carrying only a pointy stick and a trash-can lid.

Then we heard the noise.

"What was that?" whispered Eleven Evelyn.

"Maybe it was another one of the contestants."

"I've worked in the Cavalcade for three years now," said Eleven Evelyn. "I know what contestants sound like. That wasn't one of them."

We heard it again.

It was a scratching, clicking sort of sound. It was getting closer.

"Listen," I said to Eleven Evelyn.

"I am listening."

"Do you hear that?"

"Yes. Voices."

I could hear a whispered conversation taking place somewhere close. It sounded like they were having an argument, and just barely able to keep from shouting at each other.

"Hello," I called.

The voices stopped.

"Is one of you the Beast of the Mall?"

I heard the voices again. "Tell her," one of them said.

"No," said the other one. The voices were coming from behind an abandoned pretzel stand.

"Tell her!"

"Tell me what?" I asked.

The pretzel stand shook. From behind it crawled two Moon Cockroaches, looking guilty.

Eleven Evelyn took a step back. "Roaches! In the mall!"

They stood up, and I could see the "Hello!" stickers on their thoraxes. It was Delaney and Harmonic Convergence Saa.

"Hi, Theora," said Delaney.

"What are you doing here?" I asked.

"We are really sorry," said Harmonic Convergence.

"Dude, we are so sorry. Sorry sorry sorry. Think of the sorriest thing in the universe and then add one, and that's us."

All of a sudden, there was a knot in my stomach. "Where's Verb?"

18

"T hat's kind of the thing," said Harmonic Convergence.

"How much did you like your little brother?" asked Delaney. "I mean, like, a whole lot?"

Eleven Evelyn scowled at them. "Quiet! Theora is in the middle of the preliminary round of the Cavalcade of Loveliness. She can't be disturbed."

"What happened to Verb?" I demanded.

"See, now she's disturbed. Good job, you two."

"He kind of—"

"Got away from us."

"He got away!" I said. "Haven't you ever been babysitters before?"

"Well, we're used to larvae," said Delaney. "They don't move around so much."

"That's no excuse! Where did you last see him?"

"Um, around here," said Delaney, swiveling his big insect eyes indecisively.

"Maniacs!" said Eleven Evelyn. "What were you doing in the Neptune Galleria anyway? Didn't you see the warnings at the spaceport? The big posters that said, 'Please don't go to the mall'? What did that mean to you? And now look." She pointed to me. "You're making my contestant cry."

"I am not," I said.

"Well, she probably will in a minute. Thanks a bunch, you roaches."

Harmonic Convergence ruffled his wings in an embarrassed way. "It started out all right. We were at the largest ball of string on Neptune, and then Delaney mentions that there's supposed to be a lost treasure in video game tokens hidden somewhere in the mall."

"Dude, I did not. You did."

"Anyway, your brother wanted to see if we could find it."

"And you let him?" I asked.

"Well, he was our guest. What were we going to do, say no?"

"Yes."

"We drove over here," said Harmonic Convergence, "and Verb picked the lock on the maintenance entrance."

Great. Verb was going to get eaten, and Mom was going to blame me for the rest of my life.

"We were only in here for about five minutes before the little dude took off," Delaney said. "We were trying to find him when we heard you coming up the escalator. So we hid."

"All right, someone has to take charge here," said Eleven Evelyn. "You two, Roach A and Roach B."

"Delaney," said Delaney.

"Harmonic Convergence," said Harmonic Convergence.

"I don't care. You're upsetting my contestant. You go find her brother right now."

Since they were the ones who had lost Verb in the first place, this didn't sound very reassuring.

"I'll go with you," said Eleven Evelyn to the Moon Cockroaches. "The rules of the Cavalcade of Loveliness say that I can't help Theora any more than I already have, but I can at least make sure she doesn't have to worry about a missing relative." She smiled at me. "Everything will be fine, Theora. Just get out there and find that Beast. I know you can do it."

"Wait a minute," I said.

"It's all right. We'll find him."

"No, I heard another noise."

"Whoa," said Delaney. "I heard it, too."

The Moon Cockroaches waved their legs in the air. I thought they had gone crazy until I realized that insects hear sounds through special organs on their legs. You never know when science is going to come in handy.

"Hey! Hello!" said a voice. It came from somewhere up ahead, past the food court and around a corner. It was Verb. I ran, with Eleven Evelyn and the Moon Cockroaches following me.

Around the corner was one of those waiting areas that malls have where you can sit and relax while the rest of your family keeps shopping. After the mall had been abandoned, the decorative plants must have grown out of control, because it looked like a miniature jungle. Plants stretched up to touch the skylights, two stories above. The floor was covered with a layer of dead leaves that crunched when we walked.

"Where'd he go?" I asked.

"Quiet," said Harmonic Convergence. The two Moon Cockroaches had their legs extended again and were turning slowly in circles. "We're trying to hear his heartbeat."

"Can you really do that?" I whispered.

"We'll let you know in a minute."

"Hey, guys!" It was Verb again. His voice was coming from somewhere in the tangle of plants.

"Got him!" Delaney pointed in that direction. "There he is!"

"Thanks," I said. "Verb, get out here."

"I will in a second. I found something cool."

"Was it the video game tokens?" Delaney asked, sounding excited.

"Better."

"Young man, your sister is searching for the Beast of the Mall," said Eleven Evelyn. "We would appreciate it very much if you would climb down from wherever it is you've hidden yourself, so she can get her mind back on her task."

"She doesn't have to," said Verb.

"Why not?"

"Because the Beast is right here," said Verb.

"Hey there," said a voice from the dark forest.

"It's the Beast!" shrieked Eleven Evelyn.

"Oh, man," said Delaney.

"Verb! Get over here! Now!"

"It's all right," said Verb, "he's friendly."

"I am," said the Beast.

"His name is Claude, and he has to get to Earth," said Verb, stepping out of the shrubbery. He waved at something in the shadows. "Come on out, she's okay."

"Thank you kindly, but I think I'll stay put for the time being." I almost thought I recognized the voice, but I couldn't place it.

"Come on. They're not going to hurt you." Verb sounded like our mother does when she's trying to persuade him to go quietly to the orthodontist. It never works for Mom, so I don't know what Verb was expecting to achieve.

"It's not that I doubt your word, little buddy, but I can see that the young lady there is totin' a PS-5."

I aimed the pointy stick at the floor. "There. Is that better? All we want to do is talk."

"Be careful," said Eleven Evelyn. "That's the Beast. I bet it's crafty!"

From somewhere in the jungle there was a laugh. "Ha! You little green critters have really got the wrong end of the PS-5, if you know what I mean."

"I have to admit, I hadn't imagined that the Beast would talk this way," said Eleven Evelyn.

"What were you expecting?" it asked.

"Growling. Leaping. Eating."

"Which is fine with us," I added quickly. "We like you just the way you are." No point in giving it ideas.

"Y'all caught me on a good day. This little guy here—"

"Hi, Verb," said Delaney Saa.

"Since I've been in this mall, Verb's the first person I've met who didn't try to brain me with a frying pan or carry me off in a sack. I appreciate it."

"But you're the Beast of the Mall," Eleven Evelyn said. "The one who brings inevitable discomfort to all who dare enter the forbidden Neptune Galleria. Right?"

"All I'm trying to do is get a ride. The folks I came here with up and took off without me."

"That's why we need to take him to Earth. He's not a monster," said Verb. "He's just misunderstood."

"Why did you run off from Delaney and Harmonic Convergence?" I asked.

"I thought I saw something moving. I wanted to get a better look."

"He wasn't scared at all," said Claude the Beast, still hiding in the shadows. "Brave little soldier."

"Stupid little twerp," I corrected. "That was very dangerous, Verb."

"I know. Sorry."

"Just don't do it again." Then, to the Beast, I said, "You really can come out now."

One of the big decorative ferns shuddered. It looked like something was trying to push its way through, but I couldn't see what was doing the pushing. Then I understood. The plant was moving on its own.

"Nice to meet you," it said.

We stared.

"You're the Beast of the Mall?" asked Eleven Evelyn.

"Yep," said the fern.

"Do you have the lost treasure of video game tokens?" asked Delaney.

"Nope."

"Drat," said Harmonic Convergence.

"So when the Poison Squid Creatures abandoned the

Neptune Galleria, they left you here," said Eleven Evelyn. "They left you behind like a lethal, um, housewarming gift, to deny the mall to its rightful owners. Is that it?"

Claude waved his leaves. "Not exactly. See, I just hitched a ride with these Poison Squid people because they were going in the same direction. They ditched me in the mall, and now I'm stuck here."

Eleven Evelyn whispered in my ear, "I don't trust this vegetation." Then, louder, she said, "Do you deny that you were part of the Poison Squid Creatures' invasion force?"

"Lady, there was no invasion force. They were looking for some soft pretzels and swanky new dancing shoes. There are no good shoe stores on Pluto."

"Impossible. The Poison Squid Creatures are savage conquerors. After all, several members of the Neptune Safety Patrol were forced to take antihistamines and lie down with cold cloths on their foreheads as a result of the battle. It's all in the *Malliad*."

"They're not even poisonous," said Claude. "They have a thick mucus coating. They started calling themselves 'Poison Squid Creatures' because that sounds a lot tougher than 'Snot-covered Squid Creatures.'"

"Eww," said Harmonic Convergence.

"I reckon that their mucus might have caused some sort of allergic reaction with all the makeup that the Neptunians wear."

I looked closely at Eleven Evelyn. I couldn't tell if she was wearing any makeup.

"It's important to stay nice and green," she said.

Verb was acting very smug, like he always does when he proves himself right. "When the Neptunians thought they were being poisoned, they chased the Poison Squid Creatures out of the mall, and the Poison Squid Creatures forgot Claude," he said. "See, it was all a big misunderstanding."

"Well, if you knew we had the wrong idea," said Eleven Evelyn, "why didn't you say anything? It's not like we haven't had other Cavalcade of Loveliness contestants up here trying to find you."

Claude shuddered, making his leaves dance. "They had nets and tranquilizer darts and things. I was pretty sure they didn't want to hear anything I had to say. I calculated that the best thing to do would be to lie low for a while until folks started to come to their senses. My little human buddy here was the first one who acted like he wanted to talk things over."

"Heavy," said Delaney Saa.

"I am just sick about having been so much trouble for y'all," said Claude, "and I hate to impose again, but is anybody leaving Neptune any time soon?"

"You really don't want to haunt our mall for all eternity?" Eleven Evelyn asked, sounding thrilled. "You want to leave Neptune? We can have our mall back?"

"We've got a spaceship," said Harmonic Convergence. "We'd be glad to give him a lift."

"I'm supposed to go to Earth to meet up with my brother. That ain't too far out of the way, is it?" asked Claude.

"Dude, no problem," said Delaney.

Eleven Evelyn insisted that Delaney and Harmonic Convergence get in contact with the Neptunian authorities and let them know that the Beast of the Mall was about to become somebody else's problem. They said they would need an hour, so the rest of us waited in the gloom, making uncomfortable small talk. After what felt like a very long time, we heard the whine of an engine overhead, and then something landed on the roof with a heavy thud.

"Let's go," I said.

Up on the roof, the wind was cold. It whipped Claude's leaves around and sent the rings on Eleven Evelyn's helmet wobbling unsteadily. Once again, I wished I had picked up my jacket before leaving the house this afternoon. I glanced up at Claude to see how he was doing. It was the first time I'd been able to get a good look at him in the light. He was large, but I kept thinking how much he seemed like a perfectly normal plant. In the back of my mind I had been expecting to see hidden eyes and a mouth somewhere, like those scary battery-operated plastic Christmas trees that come to life and start singing when anyone walks past. But he was just a fern. Except for the talking, and being able to move around by himself, Claude looked just like any regular potted fern as big as my family's garage.

"I don't know," Claude said. "I hate to admit this, but I'm feelin' a mite fearful."

"There's nothing to worry about," said Eleven Evelyn brightly. "The Neptunian people are known for their hospitality and warm welcomes."

"These are the guys who chased me through the mall with photon disintegrator beams and atomic-powered string trimmers."

"Just a misunderstanding. Once we explain everything, they'll love you, I'm sure of it."

At the far end of the roof, we saw a small cluster of Neptunians standing next to a spaceship that looked like a giant brass cockroach.

"That must belong to the twins," said Verb.

The Neptunians took a shuffling step forward. They acted as if they were afraid to get too far away from the bugship's gangplank.

Even this tiny progress was too much for Claude's nerves.

"Okay, that's enough for today," he said, scraping his pot back toward the stairs. "We can try this all again tomorrow."

Verb and I grabbed his pot and tugged in the opposite direction. It was hard work. I never would have thought that a fern, even a giant one, would be so strong. I mean, they just don't seem like strong plants.

"Hang on," I grunted. "Just give it a second. Look, we'll stand in front of you, all right?" Dragging Verb along, I put us between Claude and the others, who were still a pretty long way off. "Eleven Evelyn, come here."

She stayed behind Claude. "Maybe I should guard the stairs. You know, in case he makes a break for it."

"You're not scared, are you?" asked Verb.

"I am," said Claude.

"Of course I'm not scared. It's just that . . ." Eleven Evelyn trailed off. On the other side of the roof, a Neptunian had separated from the rest of the group. He wore a complicated metallic harness that bristled with knobs and cones and things that looked like projectors. Whatever they were, they were aimed at us.

"What's he doing?" I asked Eleven Evelyn.

From behind Claude, she said, "I don't know. This isn't how the Cavalcade of Loveliness committee usually greets guests."

"Maybe he's just going to zap us all," suggested Verb. "You know, take us out before we can do any harm."

"Oh, that's just dandy." Claude's leaves twitched in agitation.

The Neptunian had gotten halfway across the roof to us. He stopped and punched something into a keypad on his harness.

"Look out!" said Claude.

"He's going to fire!" said Verb.

Before we could duck, the lights on the Neptunian's harness glowed bright purple, and it made a flat, bleating sound.

No one moved.

"That was it?" asked Verb.

The Neptunian punched the keypad again. This time, the harness played four sounds, rising in pitch while the lights changed colors. I recognized the sounds from band class: they were part of a musical scale.

I couldn't believe what was happening. "I get it," I said. All of a sudden, the green guy in the harness wasn't so scary. "Didn't we see a movie about this once?" I asked Verb. "Where the aliens try to communicate with musical notes?"

"That's not the way you're supposed to do it," said Verb. "The *Übermind Technical Manual* says that if you ever meet an extraterrestrial, you're supposed to use mathematics to communicate. You're supposed to count off the first five prime numbers so they know you're intelligent."

I told him to be quiet. The Neptunian must have gotten tired of waiting for us, since he was rapidly punching in a new code. This time, instead of notes, his musical harness played a beat: tap-tap-crack, tap-tap-crack.

"Okay, let's get this taken care of." I was pretty sure I knew what he was looking for, so I took the blunt end of the PS-5 and tapped out a beat on Claude's pot.

Crack-t-tap-tap, crack-t-tap-tap, crack-t-tap-tap.

"Ow!"

"Sorry, Claude. Can you wave your leaves back and forth?"

"You know, technically, they're fronds."

"Whatever."

"Right. Sorry." Claude swayed back and forth while I kept tapping out the beat. The Neptunian watched us for a bit, then turned around and waved at the rest of his group by the bug-ship.

"It's all right," we heard him yell. "They've got rhythm!"

"Please excuse us for having to test you with the Musical Mind Meter," said the chief of the Neptune Safety Patrol. "We had to make sure you weren't savages."

I nodded over to where Delaney Saa and Harmonic Convergence Saa were scarfing cheese cubes from the buffet table. "Didn't those two tell you what was going on?"

The chief made a face. "Well, yeah, but look at them."

"I see your point."

We were standing in the second-best ballroom in the Hall of Contestants, in the middle of a party celebrating the end of the Beast of the Mall. Hundreds of Neptunians were there, as well as lots of Cavalcade of Loveliness contestants, all of whom looked a little jealous. Eleven Evelyn was surrounded by Neptunian newspaper reporters, and Verb and Tsam were standing by the ice sculpture. Verb was offering a cup of Neptune Punch to Claude. There was a wide empty space around Claude, as if everyone was still half-afraid that he was going to pounce on someone.

"Miss Earth!" The MC5000 rolled up and shook my hand. "I think I can speak for all of Neptune when I say that we owe you an immense debt of gratitude for defeating the horrible Beast of the Mall."

I had explained this a dozen times, but nobody was listening. "I didn't really defeat anybody," I said.

"Same difference," said the chief. "We're just glad to get our mall back."

Eleven Evelyn had detached herself from the reporters and joined the chief and me. "This is such a lovely party," she said, "and on such short notice, too."

Ever since we'd left the roof of the mall, Eleven Evelyn

had been rushing around, making arrangements for this victory reception. At first, I was a little self-conscious about being the center of attention at a huge party like this. Once we got there, though, I saw that everyone was pretty much either talking to friends or staring at Claude, and I felt a lot better.

"You really didn't have to go through so much trouble for this," I said.

"Don't worry about it. This is a celebration! We get our mall back. Besides, this has been a pretty easy pageant for me. Last year I was the contestant wrangler for Miss Planet of the Marmaloids. Are you familiar with it?"

I shook my head.

"Let's just say that I had to send out for the extra-strength silver polish when everything was done, and it still took me a week to get my hat clean. I swear, those are the stickiest people in the universe. By comparison, this has been great. I met an interesting person from Earth, we got rid of the Beast of the Mall, and I'm still nice and tidy."

"Eleven Evelyn, there's someone I'd like you to meet." Another Neptunian, with TALENT COORDINATOR stamped on his helmet, took Eleven Evelyn by the arm and led her away.

A scaly insect claw tapped me on the shoulder.

"Hey!" It was Delaney. "Have you tried the cheese?"

Harmonic Convergence was right next to him. "Did we say again how sorry we are for losing your little brother?"

"That's okay."

"We still feel kind of bad about it."

I shrugged. "These things happen." Since the Beast had turned out to be friendly and Verb hadn't been eaten, it didn't seem like that big of a deal anymore. I couldn't even remember being upset about it, though I knew I must have been.

"Anyway," said Delaney.

"We heard a rumor," said Harmonic Convergence.

"Since this is such a big deal and all," said Delaney. "You know, a VIP reception."

I looked from bug to bug. "What?"

"We heard that Hortense Benway was supposed to be here." They rubbed their forelegs together with excitement. "You didn't happen to see Hortense Benway, did you?"

"Sorry, guys," I said.

"You're sure?"

"I think I would have remembered."

They sighed.

"Well, did you hear anybody talking about her?" asked Harmonic Convergence.

"Yeah," said Delaney. "Did you see anybody carrying a dish of ice cream? She likes ice cream. They might have been, you know, taking her some ice cream, and then you would have seen Hortense Benway's dessert in person, and that would have been, like, so cool."

I was about to suggest that the twins, I don't know, go eat more cheese or something, when they stopped paying attention. They stared over the top of my head, and one of them wheezed, as if someone was pressing the air out of a basketball.

"Dude!" whispered Delaney, standing up straighter.

"It's her!" whispered Harmonic Convergence, adjusting his folded wings.

I turned around and saw another Moon Cockroach gliding through the crowd in our direction. Even though I was still barely able to tell one giant bug from another, I could see that there was something different about Hortense Benway. It wasn't only the little gold tiara she wore around her antennae. She was more graceful than Tsam Saa or the twins, and more dignified, too, which was not something I thought I'd ever say about a roach the size of a Coke machine. There even seemed to be a little bit of a glow surrounding her.

Hortense Benway stopped in front of me. The crowd of Neptunians, pageant contestants, and other VIPs that trailed along behind her stopped as well.

"You must be Miss Earth," she said.

"Call me Theora."

"Congratulations on your excellent performance in the first round today. I hear that the judges were very impressed."

Behind her, several of the other contestants were giving

me dirty looks. Some of them didn't even have eyes, but I could tell what they were thinking.

"Thank you." All of a sudden, it struck me that the other contestants had spent years practicing how to be dignified and charming and polite at parties, while I had been playing drums in my parents' garage, trying to teach Mary Beth and Ginger how to play Pixies songs.

"This is Delaney Saa and Harmonic Convergence Saa," I said, stepping back so that I was between them. "They're twins. And they're big fans."

"Um, hi," said Harmonic Convergence, who sounded stunned.

"It's lovely to meet you both," said Hortense Benway. As she shook hands, I could tell that she was definitely glowing. Now I could hear a soft humming coming from somewhere. I wondered if Hortense Benway was radioactive.

"They were really helpful in finding the Beast of the Mall," I volunteered, since the twins appeared to be as tongue-tied as I was.

"That's fascinating," said Hortense Benway.

"Well, you know," said Delaney.

The humming noise was louder now. It sounded like an air conditioner turned up to maximum. Whatever was making that sound, it felt like it was right on top of us. Then I heard something breaking and realized that the sound *was* right on top of us.

I looked up at the wide skylight that was set in the ceiling.

"Oh, no," I said.

Hovering just a few feet above the skylight was some kind of spaceship, swaying back and forth. I could see a big purple brain painted on it and realized, with a sinking feeling, that it belonged to the Überminds.

A hatch hung open on the underside, and someone was leaning precariously out. He was holding on to the edge of the hatch with one hand and kicking at the skylight. After a couple of solid cracks with his boot, part of the skylight fell in. Broken panes of Plexiglas fell to the floor, smashing the buffet table and knocking an arm off the ice sculpture.

Naturally, this caused a panic. Everyone screamed and tried to run for the exits. The cockroach twins dove at Hortense Benway, shouting, "We'll save you!" I just missed getting trampled by one of the contestants, who had more feet than I could count.

A pair of ropes were thrown down from the hatch, and

immediately two people in white coveralls slid through the skylight and into the reception room.

This was about when I started to think it might be a good idea to get out of the way. I was a few seconds too late. One of the men from the Übermind ship touched down next to me and clipped a motorized pulley thing to my belt.

"Melvin!" I said.

He nodded. "Hang on." In a split second we were hurtling upward, being reeled in to the spaceship.

We didn't make it.

We got halfway to the skylight when the pulley froze up. We stopped with a jerk, then began to spin around slowly, like a yo-yo at the end of its string.

"Wonderful," said Melvin.

"We've got a problem down here!" someone said. It was Dr. Übermind, shouting up to the spaceship. He was on the other rope, also stuck, and he was holding Eleven Evelyn.

"Something has happened to Verb Theremin," he yelled. "He's been transformed into some sort of space creature. Alert the sick bay. Tell them to prepare the genetic descrambler."

"Dr. Übermind?" said Melvin.

"Oh, yes. We're also stuck."

"I'm not Verb," said Eleven Evelyn. I admired the way she was still so calm. When Tsam had grabbed Verb and me with his capture kite, I hadn't been half as composed.

"What did you say?" asked Dr. Übermind. "The transformation has affected the language centers of your brain! I can't understand you!"

Eleven Evelyn sighed. "Hang on." She pulled a can of language spray out of her pocket and blasted a cloud of it at Dr. Übermind and Melvin.

Dr. Übermind took a few sniffs. "Fascinating."

"Hey!" From the floor, Verb waved up at us.

Above, Johnny Übermind leaned out of the hatch. "Dad! The winch is jammed! The chemical composition of Neptune's atmosphere has affected the coefficient of friction."

"Then engage the backup winch, and hurry! We've got to rescue them!"

"We don't need to be rescued," I said.

"And I live here," Eleven Evelyn said.

"The backup winch isn't installed," reported Johnny.

Dr. Übermind glared at Melvin.

Melvin made an embarrassed face. "I didn't think we'd need it."

We hung there for a few seconds, twisting in a circle. The reception guests, the ones who hadn't run away, stared up at us, more curious than scared.

"I think we need to talk," I said to Melvin.

We sat on folding chairs, arranged in a circle around a table piled high with sandwiches and little squares of cake. After some of the taller contestants had stood on each other's shoulders to form a ladder to get us down, Eleven Evelyn had led us into the caterers' preparation room. This way we could discuss just exactly what we thought was going on without the entire reception staring at us.

I sat next to Eleven Evelyn. Dr. Übermind and Melvin were across the table from us. Verb was at one end, and I could tell that he was trying to decide whether to grab a piece of cake or not. Johnny was at the other end. On his lap he held an oversized metal helmet, which had flashing lights and a small satellite dish on it. It looked pretty odd. It had looked even odder when he lowered himself from the Übermind spaceship with it buckled onto his head.

"It's good to see you again, Theora," Johnny said.

I didn't say anything back. I still couldn't believe that the Überminds had followed us all the way to Neptune. I just stared at Johnny's white coveralls, which were streaked with paint.

He looked down. "Our regular rescue outfits were at the cleaners, so we had to borrow these from the painting crew. I hope they look all right." He laughed lamely, like he knew that what he'd said wasn't really funny. I smiled. He was right, it wasn't funny, but I wanted to make him feel better. After all, he had come all the way from Earth to look for me. It wouldn't kill me to be polite.

Eleven Evelyn and Dr. Übermind were still glowering at each other.

"I realize that you must have very different customs on your home planet," began Eleven Evelyn, "but crash-landing your spacecraft in the middle of a gala victory reception is simply not done here on Neptune."

"It wasn't a crash landing, it was a perfectly executed precision arrival," corrected Dr. Übermind.

"Be that as it may, Theora is in the middle of a closely contested pageant, and her superb performance against the Beast of the Mall has put her at the head of the field. It's my duty as a contestant wrangler to demand that you get back in your spaceship and let us get on with our work. The entire course of intergalactic beauty pageant history could be affected."

Dr. Übermind cleared his throat. "Theora is a citizen of the planet Earth, and more important than that, she is a fully enrolled member of the Übermind Junior Research Institute. As such, she is under my protection and is not eligible to be kidnapped by space creatures and dragged off to some nameless planet for some nameless purpose."

"Neptune is *not* nameless! And I'll have you know that there is no better opportunity for young females of outstanding character than the Cavalcade of Loveliness! Did you know that in the past hundred years, twenty-three of our contestants have gone on to be elected to the Galactic Council of Elders, forty-one are heads of major corporations, nineteen have been named Most Beautiful Thing in Space, and four have started in the Pro Bowl of Theoretical Physics?"

"That's impressive," said Melvin.

"And speaking of space creatures, I'll have you know that I'm the only normal one here," said Eleven Evelyn. "*You* gentlemen are the space creatures. You don't see *me* complaining."

"The Neptunians didn't even kidnap us," added Verb. "That was the Moon Cockroaches."

Dr. Übermind blinked. "Pardon me?"

"Forget it," I said. There was no need to make things any more complicated than they already were. "No one has been kidnapped. I'm sorry Verb and I didn't get a chance to let you know what had happened to us, but we're fine, really. I'm also sorry you had to come all this way, but I agreed to do this, so I want to stay here until the pageant is over."

"Good for you," said Eleven Evelyn.

Dr. Übermind looked sideways at me, then at Eleven Evelyn, and said, "Obviously, she's been brainwashed."

"What?"

"Johnny, what does the mental energy scanner say?"

"I have *not* been brainwashed!"

"This may come as something of a shock to you, Theora,"

said Melvin, "but that is exactly what a brainwashed person would say."

"But—"

"The readings are clear," said Johnny. He had put on his ridiculous helmet and was leaning so that the satellite dish pointed in my direction. "Theora and Verb both have green lights on the Mind-Control Spectrum Analyzer."

"Neat," said Verb. "Is your hat a new invention?"

"Sort of." Johnny took it off and showed it to Verb. "I've been working on it for a while now, ever since we tangled with that gang of industrial spies who had built an android Phil Collins."

"*The Mystery of the Duplicate Drummer*," I said, beating Verb to the punch. I had borrowed that one from him and read it because of the title. Aside from Phil Collins, there wasn't anything in the book about drumming. I had been disappointed.

"That's right," Johnny said. "This scanner can tell you all sorts of facts about a person's mind. If you concentrate hard enough on a particular person, it can even point you in their direction." He sounded so excited about his big geeky hat that I couldn't help being impressed. A little bit, at least.

Verb was impressed, too. "Are you saying that it has a brain-wave energy locator? You can really do all that stuff?"

Johnny nodded. "Yeah. It's a breakthrough. After you and Theora were carried off by the tarpaulin bat, I thought this would be a perfect opportunity to try it out, so we flew back to Übermind Island and picked it up. I put it on, and then I started thinking about Theora."

Johnny turned pink and didn't look at me. Instead, he focused on his hat story.

"Every time we tried to get a location, though, the indicator kept pointing straight toward the sky. We thought the curvature of the earth was throwing off the reception, so we went up to the space station to try it out. That's when we realized it must have been directing us toward Neptune all the time. So we attached the experimental hyperspeed engine to the *Interplanetary Irene* and headed this way."

"This is all intensely fascinating," said Eleven Evelyn, straightening her own odd-shaped helmet, "but Theora really must get back to the reception." She checked her clipboard. "By my count, there are still sixteen judges with whom she hasn't shared a charming anecdote yet."

Dr. Übermind stood up. "I don't think you appreciate the gravity of the situation. It looks very bad when a research institution starts to lose its members to kidnappers from outer space."

For a minute I thought they were actually going to get into a fight right there by the sandwiches, but the door swung open and Tsam poked his head in.

"Excuse me. Did Hortense Benway come in here with you?" Tsam didn't look well. His antennae were twitching, and he kept fiddling with his tie.

Verb took a quick glance under the table. I couldn't tell if he was being sarcastic or if he was genuinely trying to help.

"Nope," he said.

Dr. Übermind, Melvin, and Johnny were staring at Tsam with awestruck expressions. "What is that?" asked Dr. Übermind, choking out the words.

"Remember the Moon Cockroaches?" I said. "We'll explain in a second."

"Oh, man," said Tsam. "Oh, man, oh, man."

"Can we help you with something?" asked Eleven Evelyn.

"It's Hortense Benway. What with all the drama and the excitement, and, you know"—he waved in the direction of the Überminds and Melvin—"Hortense Benway isn't with her entourage anymore."

"What are you saying?"

"She's missing!"

Tsam was right. Hortense Benway, current Princess of Neptune and intergalactically famous Giant Singing Cockroach, was gone. So was everybody else.

"When they saw that Hortense Benway was gone, they took it as a sign that the party was over," explained Tsam.

"Can you blame them?" asked Delaney. He and his twin were poking through the rubble as if they expected to find her underneath an overturned table or the remains of a flower arrangement.

"How do you know she's missing?" I asked. "Maybe she just got tired of the party and left."

"I thought so, too, at first, but then I found . . . this!" Tsam held out a wiry gold trinket. It was Hortense Benway's tiara.

Eleven Evelyn gasped. "Where did you find that?"

"It was under the punch bowl. Don't you see what this means?"

"Of course," Eleven Evelyn said, horrified. "No Princess of Neptune would ever abandon her official tiara of office."

"Not unless she was forced to," said Tsam. "By foul play."

"Beastly foul play." Eleven Evelyn hooked the tiara on her belt and scanned the room. "Speaking of which, where is the Beast of the Mall?"

"Don't even think about it!" Claude bumped forward from where he was hidden among the decorative plants. "I didn't have anything to do with this mess, you hear? In fact, I had gone back here to catch a little shut-eye. Parties never do much for me, you know. When I woke up, everybody was gone."

"A likely story." Eleven Evelyn was not convinced.

"Excuse me," said Dr. Übermind. "I don't mean to interrupt, but who is this Hortense Benway person? And why is this fern speaking to us?"

While Eleven Evelyn and the twins explained to the Überminds how Verb and I had gotten here, what we had done in the mall, and why this was such a big deal, Tsam led me over to the other side of the room.

"I have a theory," he whispered. "Do you remember what it says in the official Hortense Benway biography?"

I had to remind him that I had never heard of the entire Moon Cockroach civilization, let alone its most famous member, until just this afternoon.

"Anyway, there's this part in it where she's talking about whenever she feels sad or stressed out or some negative thing like that, she always goes back to the little farm on the outskirts of Bobopolis, our capital city, where she used to spend summers as a larva."

"They have farms on the moon?" asked Verb, who had tagged along behind me. "What do they grow?"

"Moon potatoes," Tsam answered. "Hortense Benway, besides being lovely and talented, is the heir to the Benway Moon Potato Chip fortune."

"Oh."

"My thought is that, with her returning to the Cavalcade of Loveliness, and the pressure of her big musical number tomorrow, and then the chaos at the party, she might have gotten really stressed out. I think she took off for home." He folded four legs over his chest. "How about that?"

I was afraid to tell him what I really thought. It was true that I had met Hortense Benway for only about fifteen seconds before the Überminds arrived, but from what I saw, I didn't think she was the type of person who would get a panic attack and disappear without telling anyone.

Before I could come up with a way to tell him nicely, Verb had already chimed in and said what a great idea it was.

"Just think of it," said Tsam. "If we track down Hortense Benway at her family farm, suffering from exhaustion and fatigue, what kind of an interview would that make? *Thrilling Cockroach Tales* would flip!"

He whistled through his mandibles. Delaney and Harmonic Convergence jumped up and scurried over.

"Bring the ship around, guys," said Tsam. "We've got to make a run to Bob."

A little while later we were back on top of a roof again, this time at the Hall of Contestants, watching the twins' bug-shaped spaceship settle in for a landing beside the Überminds' *Interplanetary Irene*.

"Boy, I hope they gassed it up already," said Tsam. He was pacing back and forth with excitement. "I want to get out to Bob before someone else comes to the same conclusion I did."

I shook my head, but I didn't say anything. After all, it wasn't as if I had a better idea.

The twins' ship settled down gently on its six brass legs, barely squeezing in between the Überminds' ship and the upper stories of the Hall of Contestants. The twins didn't seem to think twice about parking wherever they felt like, even though I had seen spaceship parking lots everywhere since we had gotten to Neptune. I wondered if it was an extra benefit for people involved in the Cavalcade of Loveliness, or if Delaney and Harmonic Convergence just didn't care.

"Are you sure this is going to be okay?" I asked Eleven Evelyn. Just like the Überminds and Verb, I was interested in seeing the home of Moon Cockroaches, but I was concerned about making it back in time for the second round of the pageant tomorrow.

"Don't worry. Your scores from today were so good that you don't have to participate in the Breakfast Cook-Off Elimination Round. That's going to take up the whole morning. You'll be back in plenty of time."

"Great," I said.

She adjusted the tiara that still hung from her belt. "I'll stay here and make a few discreet inquiries about what may have happened to Hortense Benway. You know, just in case your friend is dead wrong about all this."

At her side, Claude coughed and rustled his fronds.

Eleven Evelyn rolled her eyes. "Of course, Claude will be helping me because he is so very concerned about the success of our pageant and the well-being of Hortense Benway."

"Look, I hate to be a hardwood about this," said Claude, sounding like he'd been arguing this point with Eleven Evelyn for a while, "but I know what's going to happen if I take off and this Benway chick really is missing."

"I think you're not giving the citizens of Neptune enough credit."

"I got stuck in your mall, and y'all chased me with sticks and wrote a poem about it. If I don't hang around and help out, I'm gonna get blamed. I'll be a scape-fern, so to speak."

The twins were standing at the top of the bug-ship's extended gangplank. Delaney blew a whistle. "All aboard!" he shouted. "Express service to Bob!"

"Nonstop, baby, nonstop!" said Harmonic Convergence.

Tsam grabbed as many people as he had free legs. "Let's go! Come on, move! Move! Move!"

"Goodbye," shouted Eleven Evelyn, as the gangplank rose behind us.

"Take care now," said Claude.

The door closed. Inside the ship, Delaney scrambled up a ladder, with Harmonic Convergence following close behind, and Tsam shouting, "Maximum speed, guys! We've got a princess to find!"

24

While the twins climbed up to the control room, the rest of us went in the other direction, following the signs that read: RECREATION PIT. As it turned out, the Recreation Pit was a deeply sunken area at the bottom of the ladder's shaft, with a bunch of old sofas and beanbag chairs arranged along the edges. It was completely covered, floor and walls, in short orange carpeting, like the kind my parents put down in the basement of our house.

"Hey, comic books!" Verb said, finding a stack of them shoved halfway underneath the couch. That was exactly what Verb does with his comics whenever Mom tells him to put them away. I was starting to see why he and the Moon Cockroaches got along so well.

Dr. Übermind set two beanbag chairs on top of one another, making his chair the highest in the Recreation Pit. "Now that we are under way," he said, "I was wondering if we could have a conversation, Mr. Saa. You are, after all, a representative of a species currently unknown to Earth's scientific community. Would you be willing to answer a few questions?"

"I'm not sure . . ." Tsam looked uncomfortable. "We're really not supposed to talk to you guys."

"To the Übermind Institute?" Dr. Übermind asked incredulously.

"To humans."

"I see."

I understood Tsam's point. If news of the Moon Cockroaches got out, it was bound to be bad for business at Burger Buckaroo. I couldn't imagine very many people wanting to buy cheeseburgers from a company run by giant space bugs, no matter how friendly those bugs were.

"I can assure you, Mr. Saa, that this will be strictly confidential. Anything we learn from you will be used only to increase our knowledge of the universe around us. After all . . ."

"Knowing Things Is Good," said Melvin, Johnny, and Verb, all of whom must have recognized the setup.

Tsam tilted his head toward me. I shrugged.

"I guess a couple of questions won't hurt," he said. "Just keep it under your hats, okay?"

"Excellent! Melvin, I believe you have the questionnaires and an all-species pen. Johnny, don't forget to activate your recorder watch. This is, after all, a historic moment. It must be fully documented."

I left them to their interview and went to explore the rest of the ship. To tell the truth, it was a lot more interesting on the outside than on the inside. Most of it was just plain metal corridors and storerooms and graffiti in Moon Cockroachese. The only highlight of my tour was the control room. Delaney and Harmonic Convergence both sat in overstuffed leather cockpit chairs and were manipulating switches, dials, levers, and foot pedals with all six legs. At first I thought they were piloting the ship, but then I saw the black-and-white screen under the windshield. On it, dozens of spinning, flashing lines were sliding in different directions, bouncing a glowing dot back and forth.

"Are you playing Pong?" I asked.

"Moon Pong," said Harmonic Convergence, not looking up from the screen. "It's very complicated."

Delaney slapped a row of levers, and the dot rocketed across the screen into Harmonic Convergence's goal. The screen flashed SCORE 15–12—GAME OVER.

Delaney waved his legs with joy. "Ha! I win! Who does dishes tonight? You do! Ha!"

"Stupid game," Harmonic Convergence mumbled. "Moon Pong II is a lot better."

I saw that Neptune wasn't even a green disk in the rearview mirror anymore. I wondered how fast we were going. "How long will it be until we get to the moon?"

"No time at all." Delaney patted the console and looked proud of himself. "This baby's got the off-road package."

"In fact, it looks like we're getting close to Bob's interplanetary tracking zone," said Harmonic Convergence, checking a readout. A yellow light flashed on. "There's the signal from the harbormaster."

"Um, guys, are you out there?" said a voice from over the bug-ship's radio.

"Requesting permission, to, like, land, okay?" said Delaney.

"Sure. Can you do us a favor, though? Would you mind if the robot tugboats gave you a tow down to space dock?"

Delaney's antennae stood straight up. "Dude, I think we can drive our own spaceship!"

"It's not that," said the harbormaster. "It's the robots. They're upset."

"Aww," said Harmonic Convergence.

"Yeah, a little while ago, some freak came tearing through our orbit at about fifty million Vultors per second, right through the robot tugboats' holding pattern."

"Most heinous!" said Delaney sympathetically.

"He landed real quick, scooped up a bunch of potatoes from some field, and zipped off again," said the voice. "It's got the robots all freaked out. I'd like to give them something to do."

"Well, if you put it that way, I guess it's cool. But make sure they don't tell anybody, because we're on a secret—

Wait a second." A second yellow light had started to flash on the console. "Can we put you on hold? We've got another call coming in."

"Neptune calling, Neptune calling," said a new voice. "Am I reaching Verb Theremin, or those cockroach guys, or anybody?"

"Claude!" I said.

"We hear you," said Harmonic Convergence.

"All right. Hey, y'all, listen, that little green Eleven Evelyn lady wanted me to get hold of you. Emergency's over. It looks like they found Hortense Benway."

Delaney and Harmonic Convergence high-fived.

"Really?" I asked.

"That's what they say. She wants you to get on back here so you can be ready for the next round."

"We're on the way!" said Harmonic Convergence. "Delaney, you get back to the harbormaster and tell him to make our apologies to the robots. Theora, go tell everybody the good news."

When we got back to Neptune, landing in a public parking lot this time, the first person we saw was a Neptunian carrying a roll of posters and a bucket of glue.

"Where is everybody?" asked Tsam. "A couple of hours ago, this place was packed."

"Busy, busy, busy. We're all busy," said the Neptunian. "Haven't you heard? A special last-minute change to the Cavalcade of Loveliness program. Hortense Benway has decided that she doesn't want to do just one song. She's going to put on an entire concert!"

The twins gasped and clutched each other's arms for support. Tsam twisted his tie. I could tell he was trying to figure out how best to fit this into the story he was going to write.

"She wants lots of extra promotion," said the Neptunian, who had put down his things and was slopping glue onto a wall. "She says she wants this to be a major cosmic entertainment event. Even bigger than the Cavalcade of Loveliness, if you can believe that."

"The mind boggles," said Tsam.

"That's why there's nobody around. We're all trying to get things just the way she wants them." He unrolled a poster and stuck it onto the wall. "Because, you know, no one wants to disappoint Hortense Benway."

This time it was my turn to gasp, and to clutch something for support. Unfortunately, I wasn't looking, and the first thing I found was Verb's neck. He squealed and ducked out of the way. It didn't matter. My attention was focused completely on the poster in front of me. It read "Hortense Benway" across the top, and "Live and in Concert" across the bottom, but the picture in the middle was definitely not Hortense Benway.

It was a picture of Mr. Pinweed, my science teacher, wearing a pair of fake plastic antennae and Hortense Benway's gold tiara.

"Something about her looks different," said Tsam.

"*This* is your famous singing cockroach from the moon?" asked Dr. Übermind.

Obviously, this was not Hortense Benway. Before the Neptunian poster hanger could move off, I stopped him. I pointed to Mr. Pinweed's face. "Who is that?"

"Don't you watch TV? That's Hortense Benway."

"This?" My finger was on Mr. Pinweed's nose. "This is Hortense Benway?"

The Neptunian's eyes narrowed. He was starting to think that there was something wrong with me.

"Okay, could you just describe her, please?" I asked.

"There's a poster right there."

"I forgot my glasses," I lied, and Verb had enough sense not to chime in with the truth.

"Well, you know," said the Neptunian. "She's tall and she's beautiful, of course."

"Could you be more specific? Like if you had to tell someone what she looked like."

"Hmm. She's got kind of a mahogany-colored carapace, and really deep black eyes, and her wings are sort of iridescent yellow-green."

"She's famous for her beautiful wings," whispered Tsam.

I pointed directly to Mr. Pinweed's thin mustache. "Does she have a mustache?"

"Eww, that would be gross." The Neptunian picked up his things. "If you're going to be disgusting, I've got work to do." He left us and turned the corner, presumably to put up more pictures of Mr. Pinweed.

"What was *that* all about?" Melvin asked.

"Don't you see?" I said. "It means that something's affected their minds."

"Something certainly has affected their minds," commented Dr. Übermind, frowning at the poster, "if they think this Benway person is some great beauty."

"That's not Hortense Benway," said all three Moon Cockroaches.

"But everyone thinks it is," I said. "They must have been brainwashed or hypnotized or something."

"That still doesn't explain how a teacher from our school is on that poster," said Verb.

"People!" It was Eleven Evelyn, carrying her clipboard and acting glad to see us. "I'm so happy that you made it back so soon. Now that Hortense Benway is doing a full concert, she wants all the Cavalcade of Loveliness contestants to participate in a special production number with her. We have to rehearse! Isn't that exciting?"

"Hortense Benway?" I asked, pointing again toward the poster.

"Of course. Who else?"

I hesitated. I didn't know what to do next, and it would have been great if Dr. Übermind or Tsam or anyone had jumped in and said, "I have a plan," but no one said anything. Worst of all, several of the people in our group were looking right at me. I guessed I would have to keep talking.

"What did Claude say when he heard about the new concert?" I asked. Claude, who seemed pretty sharp, might have picked up on something the Neptunians had missed.

When Eleven Evelyn replied "Claude who? I'm not sure I know a Claude," I started to get suspicious. Behind my back, I waved at the others, hoping they would take the hint and keep quiet. Whatever was wrong, it was pretty big, and I didn't want to tip off the Neptunians that we weren't affected by it.

"Let's get you back to the Hall of Contestants," said Eleven Evelyn. "There's lots to do. I've got a computer file of your dance steps ready for you to review."

"Great! I can study it in the Überminds' ship, if that's all right. They've got computers there that are more suited for human beings," I said, making things up as fast as I could. "That way I'll learn faster."

"Everyone learns faster with an Übermind computer," said Dr. Übermind. Johnny and Melvin nodded agreement.

"Go ahead, we'll follow along," I said to Eleven Evelyn.

As we turned to go, I stopped the twins. "Look, you guys, we don't know what happened to the real Hortense Benway, or why no one else sees what we can see."

"They're not as cool as we are," volunteered Delaney.

"I'm serious. I want you two to stay here and watch the ship. For all we know, something might have happened to the *Interplanetary Irene* while we were gone. We may need to get away from Neptune in a hurry, and as long as you stay here, we'll know your ship is okay. I don't think we can trust anyone else."

The twins saluted. "Count on us," said Harmonic Convergence.

"Great. I'll see you soon, I hope," I said, and ran to catch up with everyone else.

Back at the Hall of Contestants, everybody was excited. Posters of Mr. Pinweed hung on all the walls, and little groups of pageant contestants were scattered all over, practicing their dance steps.

The MC5000 rolled past us, and a bunch of Neptunians

with clipboards trailed behind it. "Be sure to send out those press releases to all the TV stations, radio beacons, and the major interplanetary newspapers. The ratings are going to be through the roof!" The MC5000's lights blinked furiously.

"Hey, Miss Earth! Isn't this great? Good luck tomorrow!" It was another contestant, Miss Vlork. She was about nine feet tall, was entirely mauve, and had two heads. I remembered her from the victory reception, where she had spent most of her time scowling at me and acting jealous that I had done so well in the first round. Now, though, everything seemed to have been forgiven and forgotten. Either the pageant contestants were all pretty good-natured underneath the competitiveness, or whatever had altered their minds had altered their personalities as well.

Eleven Evelyn led us back up to the roof, where the *Interplanetary Irene* was parked. Someone had already replaced the broken Plexiglas in the skylight.

"Why don't I just take this from you?" I said, unclipping the computer disk from Eleven Evelyn's clipboard. "We're all kind of tired from running out to the moon and back, so I think I could use a nap right now. I'll figure the disk out for myself later."

"Are you sure?" she asked.

"You bet."

She sighed with relief. "That's super. I've still got a ton of things to do for Hortense Benway's big concert tomorrow, you know. I'm in charge of the bunting for the new, expanded main stage. It's a lot of responsibility."

"Well, good for you," I said, as we climbed up the ladder to the ship. "I'll call if I need you."

"Bye-bye!" Eleven Evelyn waved as we slammed the hatch down and spun it closed.

"Now what do we do?" asked Verb.

"**M**elvin, get down to the engineering deck and activate the high-frequency mental energy screens," said Dr. Übermind. "Keep a close eye on the readouts. Whatever has happened to these poor Neptunians, we don't want it happening to us."

"Check," said Melvin, disappearing down a corridor.

"Johnny, I want you to go to the research deck and start scanning the electromagnetic spectrum. We've got to get a fix on how this hypnotic signal is being broadcast."

"Sure thing, Dad." Johnny went in the opposite direction.

The rest of us—Dr. Übermind, Tsam, Verb, and I—checked over the entire ship, trying to see if anyone had gotten in and done anything. It sounds paranoid, I know, but after watching everyone down in the convention center running around happily and not realizing that something was very wrong, it was easy to get creeped out. We didn't find evidence that anything had been tampered with, which was good, and I got to take a look around the Überminds' ship, which was also good. Unlike the cockroach twins' bug-ship, this one looked like they had put some real thought into the interior. A lot of it was done in shiny brushed metal, with glass portholes in the doors that had the Übermind logo etched on them. It was even nicer than the *Enormous Nellie*.

Dr. Übermind switched off the ultraviolet projector he had been using to test for recent footprints in the carpet. "Of course, it's impossible to say for certain, but I think we're relatively safe here. It would probably be best for the three of you to get some sleep." He checked his watch. "By my calculations, you've had a rough day."

"That's all?" Verb asked. "We aren't going to do anything?"

"We don't even know what happened to Hortense Benway yet," added Tsam. "We can't think about sleep!"

I agreed with him. Even though I was completely exhausted, I didn't know if I could just go to bed while all these strange things were happening.

Dr. Übermind shook his head. "Now, I'm sure you've read *The Mystery of the Radioactive Ruby*."

"Übermind Adventures Number One," said Verb.

"Do you remember what we did before we took on those jewel thieves pretending to be atomic scientists?"

"Loaded up the Übertank?"

"Before that," said Dr. Übermind. "We made a plan. And do you remember what we did before making the plan? We got some rest."

Verb nodded. "A tired brain is an invitation to bad science," he chanted. That must have been another of the Übermind Institute's mottoes.

"Exactly. Melvin, Johnny, and I will sleep in shifts and keep watch over the instruments."

"We can watch, too," I said. "We're not helpless." I didn't like the idea that the Überminds thought they had to take care of us, and I was sure Verb would like a chance to look at the Übermind gear up close.

"Of course you're not helpless," said Dr. Übermind. "These controls, however, are extremely complicated, and we don't have the time to instruct you correctly in their use. Also," he said, nodding politely to Tsam, "they have been designed with human beings in mind and would certainly be uncomfortable for you, Mr. Saa."

"Fair enough," said Tsam.

"Whatever we decide to do tomorrow, we will need all of you rested and alert. Especially you, Theora. The best thing you can do right now is to get some sleep."

So we did. Verb and I slept in bunks in the empty crew quarters, and Tsam slept clinging halfway up the wall. Before falling asleep, though, he took a small notebook and a pen out of a pocket in his exoskeleton and wrote down some notes on the day's events.

"This is going to be such a great story," he said, scribbling. "You know, if we all live."

The next morning, after I had washed my face and gotten a piece of freeze-dried toast from the food locker, I found everyone else up on the research deck, squeezed in between lots of video screens and computer terminals and electronic things with flashing lights.

"It's quite complex," said Dr. Übermind, watching a screen. "Whoever is sending out this mind-control beam, they're using a very intricate system. It's taking us much longer than we thought it would to determine where the signal is coming from."

"Did you try using a narrow-beam sweep?" asked Verb.

"Two kinds," said Johnny. "Regular narrow and extra-narrow. They keep shifting the harmonic amplitude."

"It's very frustrating," said Melvin.

On one end of the console, a telephone rang.

Dr. Übermind frowned at it. "I told the Institute not to disturb us while we were on this mission."

"Look at the caller ID," said Melvin. "That's a local call."

Cautiously, Dr. Übermind pressed the speaker button. "Hello?"

"Dude!"

"Delaney, how did you get this number?" demanded Tsam, leaning over Dr. Übermind's shoulder.

"We just called up the Earth creatures and said, 'Hey, Earth man, can you give us the number of those Übermind guys?' and here we are."

"When we get back, I want to have a staff meeting about our call-screening procedures," whispered Dr. Übermind to Melvin.

"Just wanted to say hi," said Delaney.

"Aren't you excited?" asked Harmonic Convergence. "Today's the big day!"

"What?" I said.

"Hortense Benway's big concert! It's today!"

I felt sick.

"You're joking," said Tsam into the speakerphone. "Don't you remember the poster?"

"Dude, sure I do. I snared one for the Recreation Pit. Great picture, isn't it?"

It was true. Delaney and Harmonic Convergence had been brainwashed, too. Just like everyone else on Neptune except for us. It was my fault. I was the one who had told them to stay with their bug-ship. First Claude was missing, and now the twins had been hypnotized. If they had come with us, they might have been all right.

I stood. "I have to go," I said.

"First door on the left," Melvin said, not looking up.

"That's not what I mean. I'm going to go get the twins. It's my fault that their brains got scrambled, or whatever happened to them, and if I can bring them back here, maybe we can figure out how to help them."

"Theora, wait," said Johnny. "You can't go."

I stepped out into the corridor before he had a chance to block my way. "We aren't getting anything done here. You said it yourself. Besides, I owe it to them."

I heard someone shout, "Wait! This isn't a scientifically sound decision!" But it was too late. I was already down the ladder and unscrewing the exit hatch.

By the time I reached the ground floor of the Hall of Contestants, some of my excitement and anger had worn off. Everything here was so normal and wholesome-looking that, if I hadn't known better, I would never have imagined that anything was wrong. Lots of contestants were still rehearsing their dance steps, and they looked like they had gotten better. The ones who didn't have feet had figured out how to sway or wobble or ooze along in rhythm with everyone else. The Neptunian contestant wranglers were running around with their clipboards, and they seemed to be even busier than ever.

A few seconds later, I found out why.

Hortense Benway's entourage was on the move. At first, all I saw was the hurrying mass of aliens and reporters. Then the crowd shifted and I saw the focus of their attention, Hortense Benway herself.

Of course, it wasn't Hortense Benway. It was Mr. Pinweed, in the flesh and still wearing those fake plastic antennae. As I stared at him, he turned to answer someone's question, and we were suddenly looking at each other.

His jaw dropped. Even from across the room, I could see him trying to work out not only how another human being had ended up on Neptune but how it managed to be one of his own students.

It was then that something grabbed me and hissed "Don't move!" into my ear.

There was a scuttling sound, and someone stepped in front of me, blocking me from Mr. Pinweed's view. It was Tsam.

"He's really here," I said. Up until I saw him, I don't think I completely believed that my science teacher was here on

Neptune. Sure, I had seen the posters, and we had talked about it, but somewhere in the back of my mind, I didn't think it could be true.

"What is Mr. Pinweed doing here?" I asked. I didn't expect an answer, but I couldn't keep the questions to myself. "How did he get here? What does he want? Why in the world is he pretending to be Hortense Benway?"

"We don't know," said Verb, who was slowly pulling me back down the hall while Tsam shielded us. "We don't know any more than you do."

Mr. Pinweed didn't call for anyone to stop us, and the entourage that surrounded him kept moving, steering him through the doors and out of the Hall of Contestants. He probably thought that, whatever the reason for my being here, I was hypnotized just like everyone else.

"Please don't run off like that anymore," Verb said, as he and Tsam led me back up to the roof.

"But I need to go see the twins."

"Theora, we don't know what causes this mind control. We may be in danger just walking around out here."

"I know, but . . ."

"It won't do them any good if you get zapped, too," said Tsam. "We've got to be patient. It's all we can do."

He was right, but it didn't mean that I felt any better about what had happened to the twins. It still made me want to cry. When we were going up the last flight of stairs, Verb patted me on the shoulder a couple of times. I squeezed his hand.

Fortunately, when we got back to the Übermind ship, there was some good news.

"That confirms it," Johnny said, taking off a pair of headphones and circling a spot on a map. "The mind-altering transmissions are coming from that location."

Tsam ran his antennae over the map. "That's right next to the Neptune Coliseum. That's where Hortense Benway is performing. I saw it on one of the big posters."

"The way they kept shifting their broadcast modes, it took forever to localize the signal, but there's no doubt about it now."

"You know, just about all of the TV and radio transmitters on Neptune are located over there," said Tsam. "That's probably where we should have started looking in the first place."

This earned him an aggravated look from Melvin and Johnny.

"Be that as it may, we know now," said Dr. Übermind. "Melvin and I will go to investigate the source of these transmissions and cut them off. The rest of you will wait here until we give you the signal that it's safe." He turned to Johnny. "Monitor standard Übermind frequency 603.4."

"Hold on," I said. "You just told me that I couldn't go running off to help the twins because it wasn't safe. What makes you think it'll be any safer for you?"

Dr. Übermind opened a cabinet. "Because we have these." He took out two helmets. If I thought Johnny's satellite-dish helmet had been strange, it was nothing compared to these. At first they looked like unbelievably large bike helmets, but then I saw that the inside part was designed for normal-sized heads. The outer part, the padding, was at least two feet thick.

"Specially designed shielding helmets," said Dr. Übermind, buckling the strap under his chin. "Seventy-five centimeters of a special lightweight Übermindium alloy material."

"It stops all forms of mind control," said Johnny. "None of the brain-affecting frequencies can penetrate."

"It was Melvin who redesigned these helmets and made them practical for fieldwork when he first came to the Institute," said Dr. Übermind.

"You should have seen them before," said Melvin.

Bumping into doorframes and wobbling unsteadily down the passage, Dr. Übermind and Melvin left, locking the hatch door behind them.

We sat there for a few minutes, not saying anything. Whenever I'm bored or nervous, I always reach for my drumsticks. Now I realized I'd forgotten where they were. That, more than anything else, told me what kind of shape I was in.

On the control panel, a set of gauges twitched their needles, and Johnny jumped up from his chair. "It happened again!" He wrote down the numbers on the dials and transferred them into another computer. As he checked his results, he said, "Hey, this makes sense."

"What?" We gathered around behind him.

"This explains why we haven't been hypnotized. The signals that are going out from the transmitter, they aren't strong enough to control anyone's mind."

"Even yours?" Verb whispered to me. I elbowed him. I never should have squeezed his hand.

"According to the data I've been gathering, the most likely hypothesis is that there was some initial high-energy blast that actually hypnotized everyone into believing your science teacher was Hortense Benway, then every transmission after that was a low-power broadcast. Just a refresher, so to speak."

"That's weird," said Verb. "Why not just have the thing broadcasting all the time? I mean, if they'd been doing that, we would have been zapped as soon as we landed. It doesn't make sense."

"Maybe they thought everyone who was coming to Neptune would already be here, since the pageant had already started," I suggested.

"Also, a continuous high-energy mind-control transmission would probably screw up the local TV reception," said Johnny. "Nobody could want that."

Tsam stroked his chin with two legs. "So this means that the transmissions didn't affect Delaney and Harmonic Convergence. Somebody must have gotten them directly."

"But who?" asked Verb.

At that moment, we heard a knock on the hatch of the *Interplanetary Irene*. In another setting, it probably wouldn't have sounded so dramatic and ominous and we all wouldn't have frozen in fear. In our current situation, though, it was a full minute before Johnny turned on the outside video monitor.

"It's Eleven Evelyn," I said, when the screen warmed up.

"What's she holding?" asked Verb.

"Hello in there!" Eleven Evelyn had noticed the video camera and was now speaking to it. "Can you let me in?"

She was carrying some bulky metal thing that had a big nozzle on one end. It could have been completely harmless, just one of the millions of weird Neptunian devices I had seen over the past day, but I didn't feel like taking the chance.

"Theora, we really do need to practice your dance routine!"

"What's that you've got there?" I asked, speaking into the microphone and trying not to sound nervous.

She looked down at the thing. "It's a . . . It's a Holographic Chorus Line Generator. You can work on your routine without having to find a bunch of people to dance with you."

"Prove it."

"I can't. It's not calibrated for my brain-wave pattern."

"Uh-huh. Look, Eleven Evelyn, I think I'm doing okay practicing on my own. Thanks anyway, though."

"Are you sure?"

"Take my word for it," said Tsam. "She's fabulous."

"You know, I could leave it here if you wanted," offered Eleven Evelyn.

"Goodbye."

Over the monitor, we saw Eleven Evelyn's shoulders sag. Dejectedly, she carried her sinister machine off the roof and back inside. I hated to see her so disappointed. Ever since I had arrived on Neptune, Eleven Evelyn had been looking out for me, and even though she was brainwashed right now and possibly a puppet of my science teacher, I didn't want to cause her problems.

We waited. We waited to see if there was going to be another attempt to hypnotize us, and we waited for Dr. Übermind and Melvin to return.

It was around an hour later when we saw the roof-access door open again, and two men in Übermind Institute coveralls stepped out.

"Hey, they're back!" said Johnny.

"Fantastic," said Tsam.

"That was a lot quicker than I expected," I said.

"Where are their helmets?" asked Verb.

Dr. Übermind waved at the camera. "Mission accomplished. It's safe to come out now."

I think we were all suspicious. Even though it couldn't have been easy to get around in those helmets, would Dr. Übermind and Melvin have just thrown them away? It didn't feel right.

"Uh, are you sure everything's safe now, Dad?" Johnny asked.

"Of course it is. Now get out here, or you're going to be late for the Hortense Benway concert."

So it was true. Melvin and Dr. Übermind had been hypnotized. There were just the four of us left.

"We've got you some reserved seats," said Melvin. "Right up near the front. Don't you want to come out?"

"What happened to your helmets?" Verb asked them.

"We had to take them off to get through the revolving doors," said Dr. Übermind. "After that . . . After that, I can't remember what we did with them."

"Me either," said Melvin. "Something must have happened, and we felt like we didn't need them anymore."

"Someone must have been waiting for them and zapped them when they were vulnerable," said Johnny.

"Do you think it was Eleven Evelyn?" I asked.

"Could you please let us in?" said Dr. Übermind. "It's getting chilly out here."

Johnny snapped his fingers and looked pleased with himself. Obviously, he had an idea. "Sorry," he said into the microphone, "we can't come out."

"Don't be absurd."

"Seriously, Dad. There's a radiation leak."

"Then come out at once!"

"It's from one of the luminescent clocks. It's harmless to us, but we don't want to contaminate the atmosphere of Neptune."

"Good point, son. That would be rude."

"Give us a little while to clean it up, and we'll meet you at the Neptune Coliseum, okay?"

"Do you know where the anti-radiation towelettes are?"

"Sure, Dad. I was the one who invented them, remember?"

"Of course. I don't know where my mind's gotten to today. We will meet you there. Don't be late."

Once they were gone, I said, "It's up to us now. We don't know what Mr. Pinweed is planning, but one thing is clear: we've got to stop that transmitter."

"Well, duh," said Verb.

Tsam began opening cabinets. "Do you have any more of those helmets?"

"The Übermindium helmets aren't going to help us now," said Johnny. "Remember what happened to Dad and Melvin."

Tsam continued to search. "What if we tied the chin straps extra-tight?"

"Sorry. It's too risky. Hand me that box over there." Johnny opened it and showed it to us. It was filled with hollow, dome-shaped things made of black rubber.

"Suction cups," said Johnny. "Everybody take four. Mr. Saa, you'll need six."

I would have thought that climbing down the side of a building, with nothing to keep me from falling except suction cups on my hands and feet, would have been pretty scary. It turned out to be not so bad. For one thing, they were really good suction cups. They held tight to the purple glass panels of the Hall of Contestants, and they popped off easily when I needed to move an arm or a leg, making the whole thing feel as safe as climbing down a ladder. For another thing, we were too busy to be scared. Johnny had a backpack full of radio-frequency detection gear, I was wearing a tool belt with wire cutters and clamps and all kinds of things for taking apart electronics, and Tsam and Verb carried crowbars and hammers, in case we had to break something. We knew that we were the last shot. If we didn't make it, there would be no one left to figure out what Mr. Pinweed was trying to do.

There would be no one left who even knew that anything was wrong. In addition to all the other reasons, I just really enjoyed the climbing. I'd never done anything like that before, and it was such a great feeling. It was almost like floating. If we made it out of this and got back to Earth, I was going to have to try rock climbing or something.

"Everybody be careful," Johnny said. "We want to get away without anybody noticing. That's going to be a lot harder if somebody accidentally puts a foot through a window."

"You know, I just thought of this," said Tsam. "I can fly." He stopped climbing for a second and flapped his wings.

"Hey! Watch it!" Verb, who was climbing down next to him, had gotten smacked in the head with a wing.

"Could you have carried us down?" asked Johnny, who didn't seem to be enjoying the climb as much as I was.

Tsam hesitated. "I don't think anyone's ever tried that."

"Let's not waste time," I said. "There are only three more stories to go."

Once we were on the ground, it was easy to find the Coliseum. That was where everyone else was going. The streets were flooded with people, all moving in the same direction. We followed them, trying to stick to the back alleys and look like we had already been hypnotized. I didn't see any of the Cavalcade of Loveliness contestants, which made sense. They had probably been there all day, getting ready for the "Hortense Benway" concert. At Cindy Gabriel Rossetti's birthday party, it had taken my band two hours to get everything just the way we wanted it, and that was for only three people and no dancing.

I was surprised at how many different kinds of aliens there were. I saw, among others, things that looked like seven-foot-tall doorknobs, scary insect-lizard aliens that seemed to be all fangs and scales, and a handful of guys that looked like middle-aged men in red footie pajamas.

"Remember, this isn't just a local affair," said Tsam, who saw me staring. "Even without Hortense Benway, the Cavalcade of Loveliness attracts a big intergalactic audience."

Once we reached the neighborhood around the Coliseum, it wasn't too difficult to figure out which transmitter was sending the mind-control signals. Of all the radio masts and satellite dishes and weird alien broadcasting devices that I couldn't identify, only one looked like it had been assembled in a hurry, and without a lot of help. It was made from a bunch of aluminum extension ladders from a hardware store, all secured together with bungee cords and supported by a shaky tripod of wooden two-by-fours. A cable snaked up through the rungs of the ladders and ended in a big directional antenna, the kind that people have when they live way out in the country and don't get cable TV.

Next to this homemade-looking antenna, dozens of metal toolsheds, the prefabricated kind that look like little barns, had been welded together to make a sort of complex.

"Do you think this is it?" asked Johnny.

"Come on," I said. We crept up to the structure, and I carefully opened one of the doors, ready to slam it and run the other way if anything jumped out at us. Nothing did.

Inside, there were hundreds of potato batteries, those kits that you put together in school to learn about electrochemical reactions. Generally, a potato is supposed to give you only enough electricity to power a clock or a little lightbulb, but these were all connected together, and I suspected they could do a lot more than that. I could hear them humming, and there was a feeling in the air like there is just before a lightning storm.

"Don't touch anything," said Johnny. "In large quantities, electric potatoes can be quite dangerous."

"Not only that, but these must be the stolen moon potatoes," said Tsam. "They have a larger electrochemical potential. That's why the salt-and-vinegar-flavored Benway Moon Potato Chips have such a kick."

There was another door at the end of the room, and when I opened that, I saw a dark room filled with stacks of beeping, whirring electronic equipment. The flashing lights cast dancing shadows across the walls.

One shadow, though, was dancing on its own. It was Mr. Pinweed, silhouetted in the glow of the electronics.

"It's nearly ready!" he said, hopping up and down. I'd never seen him this excited before, even when he was handing out test grades.

"Now we'll see what's what! Now they'll all be sorry!" He laughed. "Who's crazy now, huh? Who's crazy now!"

(29)

Mr. Pinweed's digital watch beeped. "Oh, dear. I'd better get into costume," he said. Fortunately for us, he left by another exit and didn't see us sneaking into his control room.

"Look at this junk," said Verb, poking through the taped-together patch cords and buzzing electrical boxes.

"It's not all junk. Look." I pointed to a mixing board set up in the center of the room, with cables running out of it in every direction. Mixing boards are what bands use to control the volume of the different instruments and make sure everyone sounds right in comparison to everyone else. This was a nice one.

"That's a Schwartzbender VT220," I said. "It's one of the best mixers there is. On Earth, anyway." My band used a Schwartzbender VT3 that we had fished out of the trash one afternoon behind Mary Beth's dad's store, and even that old model was way more powerful than what we needed. A lot of professional bands didn't even use a VT220.

Johnny was running a finger along the cables, tracing where they went in the tangle of equipment. He held his electromagnetic monitoring thing in the other hand and checked its gauges as he went along.

"It appears that this mixing board controls the input and output levels for the mind-control transmissions," he said.

Verb clapped his hands and rubbed them together, like he was about to start on some big project. "So we just smash this, right?"

"Hang on." I checked the back of the VT220 and found the main output channel.

"Does this go out to the radio antenna?" I asked. Johnny double-checked it and gave me a thumbs-up signal.

On the board, I took the slider for that channel and moved it down to zero. Then I slid the switch labeled "level lock" over to the left, freezing all the other sliders in place.

"There," I said. "Now there's no power going to the antenna."

Verb looked a little disappointed.

"You can break something later," I told him. "Johnny, does that mean everyone will see Mr. Pinweed as Mr. Pinweed now?"

He shook his head. "All we did was shut off the refresher

transmissions. It will take a while for everyone's mind to emerge from the hypnotic suggestion. Of course, we could always try to rewire the transmitting equipment. Or reverse the polarity on those potatoes. That would produce a beam of antihypnotic energy that might—"

I stopped him. We had probably done enough already. I didn't want to press our luck and get ourselves blown up. "Right now, I think it's more important to find out why Mr. Pinweed is here in the first place," I said. "Somebody has to know what's going on."

Tsam, who had been silent since we got into the control room, tapped me on the shoulder. "Check this out."

We turned. Another door opened into a different toolshed. This one was lit by the violet glow of a grow lamp. Inside, we could see a huge fern, wrapped up tightly in green cellophane like it had just come from a florist's shop. Next to it, as big as the freezer in my parents' basement, was a black box. It was open on both ends, and two words were stamped on the side in tall yellow letters.

"Roach Motel," read Tsam with horror.

"Oh, no," said Verb.

"Excuse me," said a voice from the box. "Is there anyone out there?"

Tsam ran to the box and looked in. "Miss Benway! It's you!"

"You wouldn't believe how happy I am to see you," she

said. "Wait a moment. You aren't working for that odd man with the mustache, are you?"

"Of course not! Hang on, Miss Benway, we'll have you out of there in a second."

While Tsam tore apart the cardboard sides of the Roach Motel and Johnny took out his pocket chemistry set and mixed up a solvent to unstick Hortense Benway from the floor of the motel, Verb and I unwrapped Claude.

At first, Claude didn't react, even when we fluffed out his leaves for him. I wasn't sure if he was just sleeping, or sick, or worse.

"Hey," said Verb, "he's been drugged. Look!" Verb reached down into Claude's pot and pulled out one of those fertilizer sticks that people put in their plants to make them grow bigger. This one, though, had a skull and crossbones painted on the end.

"Whoa, what's happening?" said Claude, thrashing his fronds around. "Stay away from me, Dirk! Just keep your distance!"

After a few seconds, he seemed to realize where he was and who he was talking to. "Oh, no," he said, looking around the room.

"It's all right, Claude," I said. "We've got you."

"No, it's not that. It's all this." He waved around in all directions, indicating the complex of toolsheds. "If he's already built this, then he must be on the way to finishing his plan. My crazy brother's going to perform at the Cavalcade of Loveliness!"

"You're Mr. Pinweed's brother?"

This was getting weirder by the second. Claude, a talking fern, was the brother of my science teacher, who was pretending to be a giant cockroach from the moon in order to sing at an intergalactic beauty pageant on the planet Neptune.

I wasn't the only person who was confused. "Brothers!" said Johnny. "How is this possible?"

"Well, why not? I didn't say we were twins, did I?" asked Claude. "I mean, look at these two." He pointed to Verb and me. "Y'all don't look exactly alike, do you?"

"Well, no, but . . ."

"There you go."

Tsam and Hortense Benway must have seen this type of thing before, since they didn't have any problems understanding it.

"If this horrid person is your relative," said Hortense Benway, drying the ends of her legs with an Übermind-logo towel from Johnny's backpack, "first of all, you have my profound sympathy."

"Thank you, ma'am. It's hard sometimes."

"Second, do you have any idea why he would kidnap the both of us, then use mass hypnosis to pretend to be me?"

"How did you know that?" asked Johnny.

"Isn't it obvious? Who *wouldn't* want to be me? But why now? Why here?"

"It's simple," said Claude. "He's got the bug."

"I beg your pardon?"

"Show business. My brother wants to be a singing, dancing, pop music phenomenon."

"Oh," said Tsam. "I can see that. I mean, it all kind of makes sense now."

"It's been his life's ambition," said Claude. "Ever since we were kids, he never wanted to stay home in the Crab Nebula and work at the sandwich shop with rest of the family. At first, we thought it would just burn itself out eventually, the way those ideas do most of the time, but not with Dirk."

I had to interrupt. "Mr. Pinweed's first name is *Dirk*?"

"Yep. It's a pretty common Nebula name. As he got older, though, it was clear that the local talent contests and singing on the street corner for spare change weren't going to be enough for him. That's when he packed his bags and headed for Earth."

"Why Earth?" I asked. "It's not like he ever did any singing

154

or dancing there. As far as I know, all he ever did was sit in his office and teach science."

"Well, you see, Earth was just his day job. He must have picked it because he could fit in well with the natives without too much of a disguise. The real reason he was in this solar system was Neptune. On Earth, he could hold down a job and still be close enough to hear all the interplanetary gossip about the Cavalcade of Loveliness."

Tsam nodded. "I think I see where this is going."

"Yeah, it's kind of obvious when you give it some thought," said Claude. "I mean, how many great singers have gotten their big breaks by appearing as entertainers during the Cavalcade of Loveliness?"

"That's true," said Tsam. "Remember Org Fanzig from the Planet of the Yams? The Zgvrt Family?"

"Or Terry Barsoom and his Amazing Second Head?" added Claude. "Or Entertainment Unit 439?"

"Or even Hortense Benway," said Tsam. "The greatest success story ever to come out of the Cavalcade of Loveliness."

She shook her head. "I wouldn't say that. Really, the true successes of the Cavalcade are the hundreds of young women who compete every year, learning about grace and poise, and earning valuable scholarships to major universities."

Claude didn't say anything.

"But I think I see your point," she continued. "To a struggling young singer, a date to perform at the Cavalcade would seem like the opportunity of a lifetime."

"So you can imagine how hard he took it when he auditioned for the Cavalcade and didn't make it."

"That's too bad," she said. "But setbacks are a part of the job."

"That's what we thought when he wrote home and told us about it. Apparently, when you're crazy, it's a little bit harder to deal with."

"You know, you always said there was something strange about Mr. Pinweed, but I never believed you," Verb said to me. "Sorry about that."

"He wrote that he was going to stay on Earth for just a pinch longer. He said he really had a shot at the next year's Cavalcade, and he wanted to get ready for the auditions."

"That's certainly a good plan. That's how I always dealt with rejection," said Hortense Benway.

"It gets worse. His letters started sounding strange. I mean, he was always a weird kid, but these were beyond anything we had ever seen from him. He was talking about how he had figured out how to get onto the Cavalcade of Loveliness program without even auditioning, and how he was going to make sure that he was the biggest star they had ever seen. Then he'd write about a bunch of science stuff we didn't understand and, frankly, didn't care about."

"This is why basic scientific literacy is so important," said Johnny. "He was probably bragging that he had figured out how to hypnotize everyone on Neptune into thinking he was Hortense Benway. That way he could go up on the main stage and perform and no one would know the difference until the pageant had gone out on TV and it was too late to do anything about it. He'd be famous for sure."

"Gee, I think you're right," said Claude.

I'd never heard a plant be sarcastic before.

"The thing that really got our folks and me concerned was when he stopped writing letters at all. He just kept sending us postcards with 'I'll show you all!' written on the back in crayon. That's when Mom and Dad asked me to take a spin over to Neptune to keep an eye out for him. We were afraid he'd embarrass himself in a big ol' public way, and it would end up hurting the family business."

Claude shuddered. "We could imagine how that would show up in the papers: 'Dirk Pinweed Runs Amok at Cavalcade.' 'Pinweed's Crab Nebula Sandwiches Tied to Cavalcade Scandal.' 'Loveliness? Not for Pinweed Family Loon.' That's the kind of bad publicity nobody needs. My folks were so worried that they even paid the fare for me to travel back in time so I'd be able to head Dirk off before he went nuts. Then I caught a ride with those Poison Squid guys, and, well, y'all know the rest."

"Your family runs the Pinweed's Crab Nebula Sandwiches

franchise?" asked Hortense Benway. "How interesting. Have you ever thought about serving Benway Moon Potato Chips?"

From somewhere outside the complex of toolsheds, I heard the roar of a crowd.

Hortense Benway checked a clock on the wall. "That's probably the opening act going onstage."

"We don't have much time," said Claude.

We ran across the street, dodging through the last few stragglers who were filing into the Coliseum.

"This way!" said Hortense Benway, leading us around to the back. "We can use the artists' entrance!"

At the other end of the Coliseum, we saw a bunch of trailers and flying saucers and other cargo-hauling vehicles, all parked in a cluster around a wide tunnel.

"They move stage equipment in and out through here, too," said Hortense Benway. "This will take us up into the backstage areas, and if we're lucky, we'll be able to find this Pinweed person before he goes and makes a mockery of the Cavalcade of Loveliness."

"That would be a great headline, too," mumbled Claude, as we navigated through all the parked ships. "Pinweed's Crab Nebula Sandwiches Mocks Beloved Television Event."

"Hold it right there!" A Neptunian in a yellow metallic jumpsuit stepped out in front of us, just a few feet from the tunnel.

"Could you excuse us, please?" asked Hortense Benway. "We're in very much of a hurry."

"You're going the wrong way," said the Neptunian. The word "Security" was stenciled on his jumpsuit, and the name "Nine Wally" was sewn on a patch over his pocket.

I could hear music. The opening band was playing their set. It sounded like pretty generic boy-band dance-pop stuff. They probably had a backing tape instead of real musicians.

"I don't think you realize who I am," said Hortense Benway.

"I know exactly who you are," said Nine Wally. "You're a bunch of nutcases who think you'll be able to sneak in the back way and see Hortense Benway for free."

She hissed with displeasure and drew herself up to her full height. "Sir, I *am* Hortense Benway."

"Not a chance, dollface. I just saw Hortense Benway fifteen minutes ago, and you don't look a thing like her."

Behind me, Verb whispered to Johnny, "Why isn't the mind control fading away?"

"I told you, it's going to take time."

"Isn't there anything we can do?" Verb asked.

"I'll tell you what you can do," said Nine Wally. "You can go back home and watch it on TV, and quit bugging me. If you hurry, you won't miss her first song."

"This—is—intolerable!" shouted Hortense Benway.

I remembered when Frank Black was playing at last year's Phil Phestival and I tried to sneak around behind the stage. One of the security guys had stopped me and escorted me back to my seat. There was no reasoning with that guy back then, and there was no reasoning with Nine Wally now. They've got their orders, and nothing in the world is going to convince them to give you a break.

This time, though, things were a little different. At the Frank Black show, the security guard had been about eight feet tall with muscles like a comic book superhero's. This time, he was shorter than Verb and just as skinny. I picked up Nine Wally and dumped him in a nearby trash bin.

"Too cool!" said Verb.

"Punk rock." I dusted off my hands. "Come on, let's go. We don't have time to fool around."

We ran in the artists' entrance and kept running through the winding tunnels under the Coliseum until we could no longer hear Nine Wally shouting behind us. We stopped in an alcove, breathing heavily and wondering where to go next.

"Here, take these." Claude handed out a laminated card, punched and strung through with a cord, to each of us. "Backstage passes. While the security man was busy arguing with y'all, I swiped a mess of these. I was going to pull them out from behind my back and say that we were authorized to be there, but then you tossed him in the garbage."

"Yeah, sorry," I said.

"Don't be. Mighty fine quick thinking."

"It was very impressive," said Johnny. I thought he did look a little impressed, which was not bad.

Hortense Benway was still in shock from the security guy calling her "dollface."

"As if it weren't enough that I've been kidnapped, stuck to a piece of cardboard, and impersonated by a deranged amateur hungry for exposure," she said, "I'm now being challenged by security personnel like some sort of gate-crasher. I will not stand for any more of this! Do you hear me?" She sounded like she was close to exploding.

This was the kind of beauty queen behavior I remembered from the Miss Phil Phestival pageant. Fortunately, Tsam was able to talk her down a little so we could move on.

He gave her a handkerchief, which she rubbed along her sides while making an odd snorting sound. I wasn't surprised. Insects breathe through air vents on their abdomen, so she was probably just blowing her nose.

"It's all right, Miss Benway," said Tsam. "We'll get it all straightened out, believe me."

"I just don't know what to believe anymore."

"If you could tell us where the performers will be going onstage, that would be a great help."

Hortense Benway snorted once more and pointed down the tunnel to our left, where a dim light was shining at the far end. We ran.

When we were halfway along, the music that had been playing over our heads stopped, and we heard a small rumble of polite applause from the crowd.

"Short set," I said.

"They know the crowd wants the headliner," said Tsam. "Their contract probably said they could only play for ten minutes."

"But I bet they earned it," Claude commented. "I bet *they* auditioned for this and won the job. They didn't hypnotize an entire planet and set out on some fool stunt that was going to make laughingstocks out of their whole families."

We had reached the end of the tunnel. In front of us, a wide ramp led up out of the lower levels, and we could see the vast audience out in the Coliseum. It was like coming up from underground and seeing the sky, except that this sky was made entirely of people.

"The opening act is coming off," said Johnny.

Six Neptunians hurried down the ramp, each one pulling

a large red wagon, and in each wagon was a tall mound of blue fur.

"Oh, man," said Tsam, "they got the Cerulean Six. Those guys are really going places."

Other Neptunians ran out and threw towels over the lumps of fur, and then all of them went on down another tunnel and out of sight. I never saw any of the lumps of fur move.

"I'm kind of sad we missed those guys," Tsam continued. "They're supposed to have the coolest stage shows."

Hortense Benway made an irritated chirping sound, suggesting that she didn't want to hear about it right then.

Outside, in the Coliseum, the lights went down. The crowd started to roar. I could see that many of them were waving glow sticks, and others just naturally glowed in the dark.

"Ladies and gentlemen, and miscellaneous space beings of all sorts," said a voice over the loudspeaker that I recognized as the MC5000's. "The Cavalcade of Loveliness is proud to present the reigning Princess of Neptune and a Subatomic Records recording artist—you know her, you love her—it's Hortense Benway!"

32

Music started to play. It had a lot of horns and crashing percussion, and it sounded like the opening song from a movie musical.

Hortense Benway hissed. "That's 'The Thermodynamics of Love'! That's my signature song! That person is doing my signature song!"

"He must have come on from the other side of the stage," said Verb, looking around. "We couldn't have missed him otherwise."

"We're too late," said Johnny. "He's already started to play."

Claude groaned. "Dear Mom, remember when the whole universe didn't hate us?" he said, dictating an imaginary letter.

"Stupid security guy," said Tsam. "If only we had been a few minutes earlier, we could have caught him."

"We'll catch him when he comes off," I said. "There's nothing we can do now."

"I don't *think* so," said Hortense Benway. Before I knew what she was doing, she had charged up the ramp to the stage. A second later, Tsam and Claude followed her, with Verb a few steps behind.

I looked at Johnny. Johnny looked at me.

"What do you think?" he asked.

I wanted to say "Forget it." At first I thought it was because we didn't have a plan and Mr. Pinweed would get away if we just rushed at him like this. That wasn't the truth, though. It was stage fright. I didn't want to go out there because I was afraid. All of a sudden, I realized that there was a big difference between playing at somebody's birthday party and running out in front of thirty thousand spectators.

Up above, the sound of the crowd changed. Something was going on. I didn't know what to do. Either I could go out there and see or I would have to admit to Johnny Übermind, and, what was worse, to myself, that I belonged down here.

I took his hand. "Come on."

The stage was made up of two sloping stairways that twined around a central platform and led to another door high above us. If this was like any other beauty pageant I had seen on TV, the Cavalcade of Loveliness contestants were going to parade out of that door and down the stairs at some point, probably during that big dance number I would have been rehearsing if I had been hypnotized like everyone else.

Right now, though, the focus of the audience's attention, and the target of the hundreds of spotlights, was the central platform, where Mr. Pinweed was rising up from under a trapdoor.

The crowd roared louder, and the opening fanfare from "The Thermodynamics of Love" played on. Mr. Pinweed wore a tuxedo completely covered with sea green sequins and a bow tie that flashed in different colors. His hair was slicked back, and he was wearing the fake plastic antennae, Hortense Benway's tiara, and three-inch white platform boots. It was the most hideous thing I had ever seen.

I took a quick look around the rest of the stage and didn't see a band. I was disgusted even more, if that was possible. Didn't anyone use real instruments anymore?

I did see Tsam, Claude, Verb, and Hortense Benway. They had reached the other side of the stage before Mr. Pinweed emerged. If Johnny and I looked as dumbfounded as those four did, the rest of the audience must have thought that Mr. Pinweed had found some seriously dim-witted backup singers.

Mr. Pinweed smiled broadly, like he does on parent-teacher night, and waved at the audience. The music sounded as if it was winding up the introduction and heading for the first verse. He raised his microphone and began to sing:

"My love for you is an elementary particle,
Like leptons and gluons, it's the genuine article."

This was as far as Mr. Pinweed got. Hortense Benway had launched herself from the floor of the stage, up into the air, and right into Mr. Pinweed. The two of them, in a horrifying pinwheel of wings, legs, and sequins, tumbled off the platform and landed with a crunch on the stage.

The backing tape, naturally, took no notice of this and continued to play. The prerecorded backup singers kicked in, singing "Thermodynamics, it's the law of love!" while both Hortense Benways, the real one and the impostor, lay tangled in a heap.

The crowd realized that something unusual had happened, and slowly stopped clapping, giving way to a sort of expectant quiet.

I took a step back. I would have been more comfortable behind a drum kit, but it wasn't as bad as I thought it was going to be. Still, it's an intimidating feeling to have thousands of people staring at you, trying to figure out what they're supposed to think about you. If I could have reached the microphone from where it was pinned under Hortense Benway, I would have told everyone not to worry, that everything would be straightened out in a minute.

In fact, that's what the Neptunian concert security guards did say a couple of seconds later, when a whole squad of them, led by Nine Wally, swarmed the stage and jumped on us.

"No one panic!" shouted Nine Wally into the microphone.

"Thermodynamics of love! Thermodynamics of love! Adjust your equation for the thermodynamics of love!" sang the backing tape.

Nine Wally snapped his fingers, and one of the four Neptunians who were holding on to my arms ran over and disconnected the tape.

"Give us a second to deal with these deranged fans," said Nine Wally, sticking out his chest and trying to act tough. It looked like *he* didn't have a problem being onstage.

"We're not deranged fans," cried Tsam. "We're Hortense Benway! I mean, *she's* Hortense Benway."

"Liar!" cried Mr. Pinweed. "*I'm* Hortense Benway!"

"He ain't Hortense, he's my brother!" said Claude, whose pot was being held on the shoulders of the Neptunians.

"That's enough out of you! I know what Hortense Benway looks like," said Nine Wally.

"The mind control hasn't worn off yet," Johnny whispered.

"I guessed that," I said. "Thanks."

Hortense Benway threw off the six Neptunians who were holding her and ran over to where Mr. Pinweed stood, smoothing out his tuxedo.

"Look at us!" she shouted to the security guards. "I defy any one of you to look upon the two of us and not know which of us is real and which is the filthy impostor!"

I thought the Neptunians were going to drag her away.

But it didn't happen. They paused. They stared closely at the two Benways, as if they really couldn't tell them apart.

Nine Wally lifted his helmet and scratched the top of his pointed green head. "Hang on. Which one was which?"

"It's working," said Johnny. "They're breaking free from the hypnosis."

Even the audience, who was watching all of this on the jumbo video screens above the stage, was confused. I could hear the buzz and hum of conversation behind me.

"It was so simple a minute ago," said Nine Wally, still puzzled. "One of you is Hortense Benway, and the other is a big fat fake. Darned if I can see which, though!"

"You fools!" shouted Mr. Pinweed. "It's her! She's the fake! Take her away!" He glared at me, and his tie glowed bright red. "Especially her! Don't think I've forgotten about you, Miss Theremin! When I'm famous, I'll have ways of making you sorry you tried to interrupt my debut! You'll all be sorry! Take them away! All of them!"

"Yes!" said Hortense Benway.

We were stunned.

"Take us all away!" She pointed to Mr. Pinweed. "Him too. Let us sort this awful mess out in private, away from the eyes of the audience, who deserve more entertainment than these lowbrow theatrics." She stepped to the lip of the stage, taking the microphone from Nine Wally's surprised hands.

"Isn't that what the Cavalcade of Loveliness is really all

about?" she asked. "Isn't it about coming forward, getting on that stage, and giving your best, not only because you owe it to yourself but because you owe it to your audience, those people who came out to support you no matter what the weather was like or how high the ticket prices were? Doesn't our audience deserve the best we can possibly give them?"

At this, the crowd broke forth in a frenzy of applause. The Neptunian security guards let go of us and joined in the cheering. Nine Wally wiped a tear from his eye.

Hortense Benway walked back to where Mr. Pinweed was standing, frozen with shock, and took the tiara off his head.

"Professionalism," she said, putting it back where it belonged.

The security guards rushed to seize Mr. Pinweed.

"We're awful sorry, Miss Benway," said Nine Wally. "I don't know why we couldn't see the truth right off. Don't worry, though. We'll get this big freak out of your way."

She put an arm on Nine Wally's shoulder. "Please be kind. It's not really his fault, you know. He's insane."

I noticed that Hortense Benway was a lot more pleasant when she was getting what she wanted. That, I thought, was something else familiar from the Phil Phestival beauty contestants.

Nine Wally whistled and pointed to the exit ramp. "All right, guys, take him that way."

Before they could get him off the stage, though, Mr. Pinweed gave one tremendous wriggle and threw off his captors. He ran back toward Hortense Benway, and for a second I was afraid he was going to attack her, but he pulled up short and snatched the microphone. "No one's getting off that easily!" he said.

"You've humiliated the family enough, Dirk," said Claude. "Give it up."

"Never!" He turned to address the audience. "Hortense Benway, I call upon the ancient and inviolable laws of the Intergalactic Entertainers' Code of Honor! I declare my intention to prove my musical superiority before this audience and all these TV cameras! Hortense Benway, I challenge you to a battle of the bands!"

You wouldn't think that thirty thousand people would be able to say "Whoa!" in perfect unison. Apparently, if you give them a big enough surprise, they can.

"Oh, man," said Claude.

"What's the big deal?" Verb asked. "What's everybody so excited about?" He pointed to Mr. Pinweed, who had been released by the Neptunians and was now straightening his lapels. "Why don't they grab him?"

Tsam was looking concerned. "Didn't you hear? A battle of the bands."

"So?"

"It's a challenge! Hortense Benway can't back down from that! It'll look like she's afraid. She has to show that she's the better entertainer."

Verb wasn't convinced.

"It's a musician thing," I explained to him. "Sometimes you just have to find out who's the best."

Above us we heard a roar of engines, and the MC5000 flew down from one of the luxury boxes, four jets of flame shooting out from its underside.

"Tonight just keeps getting better and better, doesn't it?" the robot said, gliding to a landing on the stage and picking up the microphone. "As the official master of ceremonies for this event, it is my duty to referee this contest, if that is acceptable to both participants."

Mr. Pinweed nodded. Hortense Benway didn't move. She just glared at Mr. Pinweed like a heavyweight boxer at a weigh-in.

The audience, still watching all this on the video screens, clapped appreciatively.

"Of course, the transgalactic standard rules for battles of

the bands will be in effect." The MC5000 wheeled over to Mr. Pinweed. "Challenger, is your band rehearsed and ready?"

"I was prepared for this contingency. My band is fully functional and lying in wait." Mr. Pinweed's tie was now glowing an ugly shade of purple.

"And the reigning champion, Hortense Benway, is your band rehearsed and ready?"

"Bring it," she said.

This must have tickled the crowd. There was more applause and cheering.

"All right! You both are allowed the customary one-hour period to tune up and discuss arrangements with your band members."

The MC5000 wheeled around to face the audience. "Well, folks, while we're waiting for the big battle, what do you say we bring our Cavalcade of Loveliness contestants out here so they can perform that super musical number they've worked so hard on? Huh?" More applause from the audience. "And since Hortense Benway can't be with us right now, do you think we could get the Cerulean Six out here to sing her part? I bet we could if you can clap loud enough!"

As the roar of the audience filled the air and a line of confused pageant contestants started filing down the stairs, the Neptunians led us along the exit ramp and into a spacious dressing room.

"We'll come and get you when it's time, Miss Benway," said Nine Wally, closing the door on his way out.

"Hey, did you see my dad and Melvin?" asked Johnny. "They were right in the front row. I think they were sitting with the cockroach twins."

Before any of us could respond, we were drowned out by Hortense Benway.

"Oh!" she moaned, collapsing onto the sofa. "I'm ruined! Your science teacher is going to humiliate me and steal my career!"

She had seemed so tough and confident when Mr. Pinweed had made his challenge. This sudden change of mood was surprising, but I was starting to get used to it.

"What's the matter?" I asked.

"Didn't you hear? This is a battle of the bands! *Bands!* I only have a backing tape. I can't go out there with just a backing tape. I'll be booed off the stage!"

"No one would ever boo you," assured Tsam. "You're Hortense Benway. The real one."

"It doesn't matter! You don't understand the Intergalactic Entertainers' Code of Honor! I couldn't back down from his challenge, but I can't go out there without a band! I'm ruined!"

Before I could say anything to calm her down, or even take a guess at what mood she might be in next, the door slid open, and Eleven Evelyn ran inside.

"You!" she said, attaching herself to my arm. "You have to get out there! The contestants are singing."

"Ruined!" wailed Hortense Benway.

I took my arm back. "I'm sorry, but I can't. I need to be here."

"But you're a contestant."

"I'm a—" I stopped. "I'm a drummer."

Eleven Evelyn gave me a funny look. "I thought we'd been over this."

"No, listen." Hortense Benway had now buried her head under a pillow and was sobbing. I led Eleven Evelyn over to the other side of the room. "Can you do me a big favor?"

Ten minutes later, we were at the Burger Buckaroo stand on the lower concourse of the Coliseum. The Cerulean Six and the Cavalcade of Loveliness contestants were still singing their musical number, which apparently was as long as an opera, and the smell of Buckaroo cheeseburgers was in the air. It reminded me that I hadn't eaten anything since breakfast.

Verb, Johnny, and Claude were back in the dressing room, trying to keep Hortense Benway from having a nervous breakdown. Now that I think about it, those three were probably not the best choice to watch over the mental health of anyone, especially someone as fickle as Hortense Benway, but I needed the others for my plan.

"Are you sure you can do this?" I asked Tsam.

"No problem," he said. "We just slip through the dimensional gateway here at the Burger Buckaroo, zip over to Earth, and pick them up."

I turned to Eleven Evelyn, who was standing with two other Neptunians, Two Hundred Marco and Seventy-four Tim.

"Are you sure these two can pass?"

"Absolutely positive. These guys are masters of disguise. No one will ever know that your humans have been replaced."

"All right, then, get going. We don't have a lot of time."

"Come on, fellas." Tsam steered the Neptunians around the counter and past the grills, back to the dimensional gateway. The counter help, a pair of Moon Cockroaches wearing paper hats, wiggled their antennae in excitement.

"We'd better get back," I said to Eleven Evelyn. "Tsam said he'd bring them right to the dressing room when he arrived."

She and I went to tell the good news to Hortense Benway: I had just sent two little green men and a giant cockroach to kidnap Mary Beth Montengo and Ginger Norton. My band was coming to back her up.

At first, when I explained to Hortense Benway that I could get my band there from Earth, I was a little worried that she wouldn't want them. We were amateurs, after all, and we had hardly any experience. But she was so grateful to have a band, any band, that she didn't bother to ask what we sounded like or even if we were any good. That was just as well, because we weren't.

Now that she had recovered from her crying fit, she was pacing back and forth in the dressing room, making a track in the pink shag carpeting. Verb had found a huge paper fan somewhere and was fanning enthusiastically to make a breeze, and Claude was holding a notebook and a pen, taking notes for her.

"I'd love to do 'Thermodynamics of Love,' of course," she dictated, "but signature songs are forbidden in a battle of the bands. Maybe I should start with a ballad, something personal, and build up from there. How about 'My Circulatory System Will Go On, Even If You Cut Off My Head'? Or maybe 'Careless Hiss'? So many choices."

"Are you nervous?" Johnny asked me as we sat on the couch.

"Of course not," I said, maybe a little more loudly than I should have. "This is great. Why would I be nervous?"

I don't know how much time we spent like that, with Hortense Benway pacing and calling out song titles to Claude, and me wanting to pace, too, but trying not to act scared in front of Johnny. It felt like forever. I think I would have been a lot more at ease if he hadn't been around, but I couldn't really tell him to get out, so I just tried to deal with it.

The door opened. It was Tsam and Eleven Evelyn, with Ginger and Mary Beth between them. Ginger and Mary Beth didn't even flinch at Hortense Benway or the big fern taking notes. This meant that either they had gotten used to the idea of life on other planets already, or they were in shock.

"Hi, Mary Beth!" Verb dropped his fan and ran over. I wasn't surprised. Verb has had a crush on Mary Beth since our first practice in my parents' garage. I don't know what it is, but all boys seem to have crushes on girl bass players. Johnny would probably start following Mary Beth around, too, as soon as he found out what instrument she played.

Mary Beth blinked at Verb a couple of times. "Hi," she said.

Ginger saw me. "Theora, are you an alien, too?" she asked, sounding like she was just waking up from a dream.

Shock, obviously.

"All right," I said, sitting them down on the couch. "We don't have a lot of time, so I'm going to have to explain all this as fast as I can."

"Oh, honey, hold on." Eleven Evelyn unclipped something from her belt and pointed it at Ginger and Mary Beth. It looked like a TV remote control with a big glass bulb on the end. Eleven Evelyn pressed a button and my guitarist and bass player were bathed in a ray of green light.

After half a second, Ginger and Mary Beth looked around, then at each other, then stood up.

"Okay, let's rehearse," said Ginger.

Eleven Evelyn waved the remote-control thing at me, then hooked it back on her belt. "It's an Expositron," she said. "Saves all that tedious work of explaining things to people who come in late."

"Wow! Can I get a look at that?" asked Johnny.

"Later, if you're good."

"Is there some gear we can borrow?" Mary Beth asked. "We went right from school to Burger Buckaroo, so we didn't have time to pick anything up on the way."

"Do you want me to find you some, Mary Beth?" asked Verb, smiling a goofball smile.

Hortense Benway stopped him. "It's all right. The terms of the battle of the bands provide us with equipment and a rehearsal room. Speaking of which, it's time we got our act together." She waved imperiously toward the door. "All the rest of you, thank you very much for your help, but now we must have solitude. You can go and take your seats."

They seemed a little disappointed, but Verb, Tsam, Claude, Johnny, and even Eleven Evelyn left us, and we went down the hall alone to our rehearsal room.

Someone had put a piece of masking tape on the door and written HORTENSE BENWAY AND BAND on it in marker. Inside was a drum kit, a guitar and bass, microphones, and cables, all set up on a chrome platform.

"How clever," said Hortense Benway, inspecting the platform. "It hovers. Once we're ready to go, they can just float it along to the stage. Very convenient."

Mary Beth and Ginger picked up their guitars, and I sat behind the drums. I was impressed. The cymbals were just where I liked them, and there were even a couple of pairs of sticks. Whoever had jumped into action when the battle of the bands was declared really knew their stuff.

"Let's just run through one quickly and see how it sounds," said Hortense Benway. "I suppose you all know 'Careless Hiss'?"

Ginger looked up. "Excuse me?"

I had wondered if this was going to be a problem.

"How about the love theme from *Endless Infestation*?" More blank looks. " 'Through the Compound Eyes of Love'?"

Mary Beth frowned. "The compound what?"

Hortense Benway turned to me. So did Ginger and Mary Beth. I shrugged, but they kept staring. I had no idea what made them think that I would have any answers.

"Okay, let's try this," I said to Hortense Benway. "We'll be here forever if we keep looking for any of your songs that we know. Why don't we play you what we *do* know, and you can use the ones you like. After all, you're a professional musician, so you'll be able to pick things up faster than we could."

I had half expected Hortense Benway to have another fit, but she was all right with the idea. Either she understood that time was tight or she liked the compliment.

We played her everything we knew: songs by Guided by Voices and the Ramones and the Groovie Ghoulies and the Donnas. We tried the Dance Hall Crashers, too, although we still have trouble with them. We even did the Misfits and Angry Samoans songs that Mom forbids us to play when we rehearse in my garage.

When it was over, Hortense Benway hadn't fainted or run out of the room crying. I thought that was a good sign.

"That's it, is it?" she asked. "Well, I suppose this is going to make an interesting change of pace for my fans. Let's hear that one song again, the one with all the shouting. I'll try to catch the lyrics this time."

By the time the Neptunian usher knocked on our door, we almost sounded decent. I don't mean to say that the band was any good, but Hortense Benway knew all the words, and she was able to fit in well. It wasn't totally obvious that we had been thrown together less than an hour before, which was as much as we could hope for.

"Five minutes, Miss Benway," said the Neptunian. "I need to take your equipment out to the stage."

We jumped off the platform, which rose into the air and floated out the door.

"One more thing," he said. "The MC5000 wanted to know the name of the band you'll be performing with."

Hortense Benway looked at us. We looked at the ground. Naming the band was still a sore subject, and no one wanted to get into it now.

"I'll just tell him your band doesn't have a name," said the Neptunian, sensing that something was up. "If you'll follow me, I'll take you to your entrance."

As we went past the dressing room, I noticed that someone was still in there. I told Mary Beth I'd catch up and ducked inside.

It was Johnny. He was sitting at the makeup table, crumpling a Burger Buckaroo wrapper and looking uncomfortable.

"What are you doing here?" I asked. "You're going to miss the show." I thought about how we were likely to sound. "Such as it is."

"I know, I just had to walk around for a minute. I was nervous."

"You're not walking," I said.

"I know. I was hoping you'd come back this way, so I could talk to you." He coughed. "I just wanted to say something before you went out. I've really had fun the past couple of days—meeting you and, well, your brother, too, and coming here to Neptune and helping you with the pageant and everything. It's been really nice."

"Thank you."

He looked around for a second, then back at me. "I guess I just wanted to say, I really like you, Theora, and I wanted to say good luck."

And then he kissed me.

There was a knock at the door. We both jumped.

It was the Neptunian usher. "Time, please!" he called.

I kissed Johnny back. "I've got to run," I said.

"I know. Good luck."

"Thanks."

I followed the Neptunian. It was probably just as well that I didn't have a whole lot of time to think about all this. I mean, kissing Johnny Übermind—it was a big deal, wasn't it? Was it?

The more I played back in my mind what had just happened, the more I started to have doubts. Maybe he was just being friendly. Then I told myself that I was nuts. Nobody kisses friends. Not on the lips. And they certainly don't hang around a dressing room on the off chance that they might run into a friend and kiss them. So what did it mean?

Mary Beth, Ginger, and Hortense Benway were waiting at the foot of one of the entrance ramps. Outside, the house-lights had gone off and the audience was clapping and whistling with anticipation.

"Where have you been?" asked Ginger.

"Don't worry about it."

"You look funny."

"I'm fine."

"Okay, places, everyone!" said the Neptunian.

He switched on his flashlight and led us up to the dark-ened stage and over to where our floating equipment plat-form had landed. There was hardly enough light to see by, but I could tell that everything had been reconfigured. The big, curving staircases and the central platform had been re-moved, and now the whole area was bare, except for another instrument platform like ours and a fence of barbed wire that separated them.

I didn't like the looks of the barbed wire, and I couldn't help noticing that the other platform was bigger than ours. I sat down behind the drums and made sure everything was still arranged the way I wanted it. The audience was waving glow sticks and clapping in unison, like they were trying to get the show started. All of a sudden, I realized that I felt great. My nervousness was gone. I was focused on what I had to do. I wasn't worried—not about playing in front of this huge crowd, and not about Johnny, either. However everything worked out, I felt like I was going to be all right. I could handle it.

A single spotlight snapped on, lighting up the center of the stage, where the MC5000 was holding a microphone.

Mary Beth leaned over the drums and whispered to me, "Why does a robot need a mike? Couldn't they just plug him into the public-address system?"

"And now," said the MC5000, "we come to the high point of our musical evening! It is my great pleasure to reintroduce the competitors in this battle of the bands. First, to my left, the challenger, hailing from the Crab Nebula, Mr. Dirk Pinweed!"

Another spotlight went on, revealing Mr. Pinweed. He had a yellow satin boxer's robe on over his tuxedo. He threw back the hood and waved to the crowd, who howled with excitement. It reminded me of pro wrestling on TV. Mr. Pinweed sneered at us.

"Mr. Pinweed will be backed up by his own band, the Interplanetary Botanical Mutant Society!"

The rest of the lights came up on that side of the stage. Ginger, Mary Beth, and I gasped in horror.

Mr. Pinweed's band was made up of cactuses. Moving, walking, instrument-playing cactuses. That wasn't the worst part, either. What really freaked us out was that we recognized them.

These were the plants Mr. Pinweed had been making us raise and take care of all through the school year. One of them, a barrel-shaped cactus with a purple flower growing out of the top, had once cut my hand so badly with its spines that I'd had to go to the nurse's office. Now it was carrying a trombone and staring across the fence at us with beady red eyes.

"I am skipping science class for the rest of my life," said Ginger.

"And on this side," said the MC5000, "a creature who needs no introduction, our champion, the one, the only, Hortense Benway!"

The crowd screamed, and the MC5000 added, "With her tonight is the Band with No Name!"

Squinting in the glare of the lights, Mary Beth, Ginger,

and I looked at each other. That wasn't bad. In fact, it was kind of cool. It sounded mysterious and intimidating. We liked it.

"This competition will be conducted according to the standard battle-of-the-bands rules," the MC5000 said. "Best two songs out of three; the challenger goes first. Take it away, Mr. Pinweed!" The robot rolled off the stage.

Mr. Pinweed pulled off his robe and threw it into the audience, and his cactus band started playing something loud and cheesy, with lots of horns and a thumping beat. It sounded like a cross between heavy metal and lounge music.

"I'm the greatest person in the world," sang Mr. Pinweed. "Anybody who can't see that is an idiot!" The rest of the lyrics were pretty much the same.

Hortense Benway came around to where the rest of us were standing. "Remember, we want to start as soon as they're done. We don't want to give the audience any chance to appreciate the performance. We've got to show them up right away."

"I understand."

As soon as the cactus horn section finished their last high note on their last time through the chorus, Hortense Benway pointed at me. I clicked off a beat, and we jumped into "Bye Bye Brain." I probably started us off too fast, but I was excited, and with a band like ours, sometimes it's not a bad idea to rush things a little bit.

When you're playing music, it's important to watch the other musicians, because it really helps to keep everyone together. Hortense Benway had to play to the crowd, so the rest of us kept an eye on each other. This meant that I didn't get a chance to see what Mr. Pinweed and the cactuses were doing while we played. If it was anything like the angry looks they gave us when we were done and the audience was cheering, that was probably for the best.

At the other end of the Coliseum, the scoreboard flashed on. BENWAY: 1. PINWEED: 0.

The audience clapped, and we congratulated ourselves. Mr. Pinweed snarled and snapped his fingers at the cactus band, who started into his second song.

To be honest, it was pretty good. I couldn't catch all the lyrics, but going by the chorus, the title was probably "They'll All Be Sorry," or something like that. This one sounded even bigger and heavier than the first one, and I tried to see what instruments the cactuses were playing. There were two guitars plus a bass, two cactuses on keyboards, a drummer *and* a bongo player, and more horns than I could count. Several of the cactuses had more than one mouth and were playing a number of horns simultaneously.

When it was over, we couldn't start right away. The applause was just too loud. I would have thought that most of the audience would have been rooting for Hortense Benway, but I guess they appreciated a good contest. I could understand that. If I hadn't been one of the competitors, I think I would have enjoyed it, too.

Hortense Benway flapped her wings, and the crowd quieted down a little. "Turn it up!" she said to us.

Ginger and Mary Beth twisted their volume knobs, and we started into "It's Like Soul Man," which is one of my favorites, and one that we can actually play pretty well.

We were just through the first chorus, and I thought we were sounding good. I was wondering if we might be able to sweep Mr. Pinweed and end the contest here, when something hit me in the arm and knocked over my snare drum.

It was a cactus! I looked over my shoulder and saw that one of the cactuses had gotten over to our side. Another, the one who had been playing the trombone, was holding the strands of barbed wire apart, waiting for its partner to return.

"Ha!" shouted the trombone cactus. "Feel free to feel fear! We of the Interplanetary Botanical Mutant Society allow no one to defeat us!"

While this was going on, I tried to keep playing the drums, but with the other cactus shaking the equipment and doing its best to push me off the drum stool, I lost the beat, and then I lost track of where the bass drum pedal was.

Mary Beth turned around to see what the heck was wrong with me, and the cactus leaped at her. She shrieked and stumbled backward, knocking over Ginger, who fell onto Hortense Benway's microphone cord and yanked it loose.

The invading cactus dived back through the barbed wire as our song crashed to a halt. The audience clapped unenthusiastically, and the scoreboard flashed. BENWAY: 1. PINWEED: 1.

"Hey, that's a foul!" I shouted at Hortense Benway. "Didn't you see what they did?"

She shook her head. "It's no good appealing to the referees in a battle of the bands," she said. "It loses their respect."

On the other side of the fence, Mr. Pinweed beamed at his mutant creations, while the cactuses jumped up and down with glee and made rude gestures at us. Mary Beth made a rude gesture right back. I was proud of her.

"We'll have to watch out for them next time," said Hortense Benway. "They know we can beat them. They're scared."

"No, we're not!" shouted the saxophone cactus.

"Does this sound scared to you?" asked the drum cactus,

and they started into their last song, "I Am Pinweed, Hear Me Roar."

"Should we go get them?" asked Mary Beth.

"Yeah, come on!" said Ginger.

"There are about fifteen of them and four of us," I said. "Do you really think that's a good idea?"

"We've got to do something."

I unscrewed the wing nut on one of my crash cymbals. "Don't worry, we will. Just keep your eyes open when it's our turn."

Mr. Pinweed finished, to a lot of cheering from the audience. He took four or five bows and blew kisses to the crowd; then he and all his cactuses turned to watch us, with their arms folded and their expressions saying, "Beat that."

We played "I Turned into a Martian," which not only has a really cool "whoa-oh" chorus but was also pretty appropriate, given that this was our first concert on another planet.

I kept one eye on the fence, and, sure enough, a couple of cactuses were sneaking through. I continued to play, pretending not to notice, until one of them had crouched to jump at me. When it sprang, I pulled the crash cymbal off its post with my right hand and swung it at the cactus, knocking it out of the air.

The crowd cheered. I kept playing with my left hand and flung the cymbal at another cactus, who ran back to Mr. Pinweed's side. Mary Beth had unstrapped her bass, and she swung it by the neck at the third cactus, who was sneaking up on Hortense Benway. It ducked out of the way, but Mary Beth chased it around the stage, keeping it occupied while Ginger and I played on the best we could. The audience went wild, and I guess I could understand why. I mean, here were Ginger and I, hammering away on a Misfits song, a big bug singing, and Mary Beth chasing a cactus in circles around our platform. That had to be pretty entertaining.

The judges must have thought so, too. When we stopped, the final score came up. BENWAY: 2. PINWEED: 1.

"No!" screamed Mr. Pinweed. "I've been robbed!" He tore at his hair, then pointed savagely at us. "Cactuses, attack!"

I picked up my crash cymbal, and Ginger held up her guitar like a club, joining Mary Beth.

"Stay back, if you know what's good for you," said Hortense Benway, holding the microphone stand like a spear.

"Then the joke's on you!" said the bongo cactus. "We don't!"

"We crave not only new forms of musical expression," said the trombone cactus, "but also . . . human blood!"

"Come get some!" shouted Mary Beth.

The cactuses rushed at the fence and started ripping it to pieces. Out of the corner of my eye, I saw that the audience was now on its feet. It had surged right up to the edge of the stage and looked as if it was going to keep on going. In fact, it looked a lot like those concert riots my mom always says she's worried about when she won't let me go to all-ages punk shows.

Through the roar of the crowd and the battle cries of the cactuses, I thought I heard someone calling my name. I turned, and a silver box came flying in our direction. I caught it with one hand. It was a lunch box, with the Übermind logo stamped on it and JOHNNY ÜBERMIND printed underneath.

I tore open the box, hoping that it had some kind of ray gun, or even a bottle of weed killer, inside. Instead, all I saw was an apple, a sandwich wrapped in plastic, a sack of chips, and a plastic tub with a seal on it.

What the heck was this supposed to be, I thought, a last meal? Did Johnny think I could fight off the cactuses with his lunch box?

"They're coming!" said Hortense Benway.

Then I understood. I grabbed the plastic tub and threw the rest of the lunch box away.

"Stop right there!" I yelled, holding up the tub.

The cactuses skidded to a stop. "No! It can't be!"

"Don't come any closer," I said. "I'll use this."

"Not the onion dip!"

It was Hortense Benway who had reminded me. She was a Moon Cockroach, and Moon Cockroaches worked at Burger Buckaroo. One of Burger Buckaroo's most popular side dishes was Deep-Fried Cactus Strips, which were served with a little plastic tub of onion dip, just like what Johnny had put in his lunch box.

"You wouldn't!" one of them said.

"I haven't had a bite since breakfast. Try me."

I took a step forward. The cactuses edged backward. I waved the tub of onion dip again, and their nerve broke. The cactuses ran away, waddling on their little cactus feet like a flock of spiky green penguins. They rushed down the exit ramp and off the stage, leaving Mr. Pinweed standing alone in the middle of all his wrecked equipment.

"Want to go best three out of five?" he asked.

It took him only a second to realize that we did not think this was funny. He dropped his microphone and ran, racing down the exit ramp the way his cactuses had gone.

"Let's go get him!" said Mary Beth.

"Yeah!" echoed Ginger.

I don't know whether I would have agreed with them or not, but it didn't make any difference. At that moment, the crowd charged the stage and overwhelmed us. It was a little scary at first, because when you're in the middle of a big, frenzied mob, you can't always tell if it's a happy mob or an angry mob, and sometimes it doesn't even matter, since they can be dangerous either way.

Several hands and a pair of tentacles grabbed me and lifted me in the air. Someone had pulled a seat out of the Coliseum's stands and held it up for me to sit in. Mary Beth and Ginger were in similar seats, and they had found a sofa for Hortense Benway, who was reclining on it and waving as they carried us away.

At one point, while they were lowering us off the stage, I got close enough to her sofa to hear her say, "This is the best thing about being a beauty queen. Of course, the scholarships are wonderful, and the lessons in grace and poise will last me a lifetime, but nothing really takes the place of a good cheering mob, don't you agree?"

They paraded us through the Coliseum, all the while chanting "Ben-way! Ben-way!" Then they took us out the main gate and into the street. We were carried through the city at the head of a procession that stretched back as far as I could see.

"This is a lot better than Cindy's birthday party!" Ginger said to me when our chairs passed each other. I agreed, but I imagined that our next gig was going to be a little bit of a let-down.

The procession stopped at the Hall of Contestants, where the MC5000 stood at the top of the steps along with a bunch of Neptunians in official-looking helmets. Claude was up there, too, waving his fronds at us. Next to him, in a cage, his sequined tuxedo ripped at one shoulder, was Mr. Pinweed.

"Got 'im!" shouted Claude.

The MC5000 flashed its lights, and the crowd quieted down.

"May I have your attention," said the robot. "In light of all that has happened this evening, the ruling council of the Cavalcade of Loveliness has decided to postpone the final rounds of the pageant until tomorrow."

The crowd clapped. It had been a long day, I thought. Everyone probably wanted to get some sleep.

"Your tickets, of course, will still be good."

The crowd clapped some more.

"Now it is my pleasure, as an official representative of the Intergalactic Association of Entertainers, to announce that this battle of the bands is over. Hortense Benway, please come forward with your band!"

We hopped off our chairs and followed her up the steps. At the top, the MC5000 took a set of gold medals from one of the Neptunians and put them around our necks.

"These lovely commemorative medallions are yours," it said. "For a while, it looked like we were seeing the first battle of the bands that wasn't going to end in a brawl, but it was not to be. We therefore salute your awesome fighting skills as well as your musical talent."

"Thank you very much," said Hortense Benway, first to the robot and then to the crowd. "Thank you all. But this would not have been possible without the support of my fabulous musicians, the Band with No Name. Take a bow!"

We did.

"Special thanks to Theora Theremin for her invaluable help in putting all of this together. Without her, I don't know what I would have done."

The crowd cheered, and I waved. I looked for everyone else—Johnny and Dr. Übermind and Melvin and Verb and Tsam and the twins and Eleven Evelyn—but I couldn't see them. I hadn't done all of this on my own, and if congratulations were being handed out, I wanted them to get their share.

"As for our challenger, he will suffer the traditional fate of those who declare a battle of the bands and lose," said the MC5000. "He must write an essay on what he has learned from all this, with special emphasis on why it is wrong to kidnap and impersonate an established singing star."

Mr. Pinweed hung his head, and I couldn't help but smile. After all the homework he'd handed out, it was nice to see him get a little of it back.

"He will also be required to help track down and capture all of his mutant musical cactuses that still run loose in our streets."

"He'll never catch us!" shouted a voice from the back of the crowd, and I saw a green shape hop away into the shadows.

"You know, when Dirk got a degree in botany, we all thought it would lead to a good job somewhere," said Claude. "Who knew he was growing his own band?"

"Our defeated challenger will also receive a free course of music lessons, sponsored by the Satellite of Gift Certificates, Neptune's favorite orbiting discount warehouse, just to show that there are no hard feelings."

"There are a few hard feelings," said Hortense Benway.

"Don't worry," said the MC5000. "It will be an extra-long essay."

"I blame my cactuses for this," said Mr. Pinweed, shaking the bars of his cage.

"Ha!" said another cactus's voice from the back of the crowd.

"They were grown with the assistance of students like her," he said, pointing at me. "Obviously, her unskilled plant care has damaged their delicate musical mutations. If I ever get back to Earth, Miss Theremin, I'm giving you an F." He gave the bars of his cage one last rattle. "Take me away, Claude."

With a sigh, Claude picked up the cage and carried it off behind the Hall of Contestants.

That was the end of the ceremony, and the crowd began to break up, swinging their glow sticks and talking excitedly as they went back to their homes or hotels to get ready for tomorrow. As the mob thinned out, I saw the Überminds and Melvin pushing their way through to reach us.

"Theora!" Johnny ran up the stairs and hugged me. Then I think he remembered that his dad and a whole bunch of aliens were watching, because he turned red and stepped back. "I'm so glad you're safe."

"Thanks to you," I said. "Without your onion dip, I don't know what would have happened."

"I couldn't get up to the stage, it was too crowded. I just hoped you'd know what to do with it."

"It was good thinking," I said.

"Admirable job, son," said Dr. Übermind, and Johnny turned redder than ever.

Behind me, I heard Ginger whispering to Mary Beth: "That's Johnny Übermind. From TV!"

Above us we heard a buzzing sound, like an immense hummingbird in flight. Tsam Saa and the Moon Cockroach twins flew down and landed next to us. The twins each held a mutant cactus wrapped up in cellophane, just like the kind Mr. Pinweed had used to hold Claude. Tsam was carrying Verb on his back.

"Hey, this isn't funny anymore," said a cactus.

"These guys were trying to break into the bug-ship," said Harmonic Convergence.

"We stopped them," said Verb. "Hi, Mary Beth."

Mary Beth was still whispering to Ginger about Johnny, who was still smiling at me.

"This is the most exciting Cavalcade of Loveliness I've ever been to," said Tsam. "Aren't you glad you came, Theora?"

I looked around. "You know, I think I am."

Delaney Saa hissed with happiness. "Let's have a party!"

The Moon Cockroach twins weren't kidding. Once we had dropped off the cactuses at the Neptune Safety Patrol offices, they led us back to their spaceship.

"Hang on a second," Delaney said, running up the gangplank. "I have to go and press the party button."

A few seconds later, an orange-and-brown-striped awning slid out from the side of the ship and unfolded itself into a huge tent. Then two metal panels on the ship's hull flipped around and revealed a pair of stereo speakers. Soon the air was full of Moon Cockroach music, which sounded like someone had added bass and drums to a tape of crickets chirping. It's not exactly something I'd want to listen to all the time, but it wasn't bad.

Apparently, I was wrong about everyone being tired. Within half an hour, the tent was full. Even after all the excitement, it seemed like no one on Neptune was ready to go to bed yet.

I'm not a very good dancer, so I don't do it much. Tonight, though, after watching the others, I figured that I could hardly look much sillier than Melvin or Tsam. I couldn't find Johnny, so I was dancing in a big circle with some of the other Cavalcade of Loveliness contestants when I saw Eleven Evelyn.

"I'm so glad I found you," she said, pulling me out of the circle. Hortense Benway was standing behind her. The Moon Cockroach's antennae swayed in time to the music, and she smiled at me.

"You'll never guess where I've been!" said Eleven Evelyn.

"Where?"

"On the intergalactic phone!"

"Um, terrific?" I said, not really knowing how to reply.

"I was talking to the head of Subatomic Records, Miss Benway's record label. He saw the battle of the bands live on TV."

I winced. "Oh, I'm sorry," I said to Hortense Benway. "I bet he's mad."

She laughed. "He loved it. He says it's an entirely new sound for me."

"He wants Hortense Benway to do a whole album with the Band with No Name," said Eleven Evelyn.

"That's right," said Hortense. "Just like what we did tonight. No ballads, no love songs, no talent."

"Hey!" Sure, we weren't great, but we did win.

"You know what I mean," she said. "Just raw noise. Isn't that dreamy?"

Eleven Evelyn beamed. "I'm so proud of you. This is what makes a contestant wrangler's job worthwhile."

"It will take some time to work out the details," said Hortense Benway. "I'll have my people give you a call on your home planet."

Before I could say anything to that, Hortense Benway was enfolded in a mass of green, leafy tendrils.

"Thank you, thank you, thank you," said Claude, still hugging Hortense Benway tightly.

She struggled to get free, but Claude had lifted her off the ground. "I take it you accept the offer?"

Claude, noticing Eleven Evelyn and me staring at him like he'd lost his mind, put Hortense Benway down and handed us a crumpled sheet of paper.

"Take a gander at this. Is this the greatest thing you ever did see, or what?"

It was an advertising flyer, the kind that come in Sunday newspapers. Half of it was taken up by a close-up picture of Hortense Benway, and it read:

Pinweed's Crab Nebula Sandwiches is proud to announce that Benway Moon Potato Chips are now available in all of our fine locations! To celebrate the addition of this new taste sensation to our menu, we will give away a free copy of the Cavalcade of Loveliness Battle of the Bands official bootleg recording with every potato chip purchase! Offer not valid in certain planetary orbits. See stores for details.

"I had my traveling publicity department whip that up," said Hortense Benway. "I just wanted to give you an idea of how it might look. Feel free to change the words. The picture should stay, though."

"My folks are going to be tickled pink," said Claude. "Well, sort of. I guess if you take this news, and add it to what Dirk did, they'll probably come out just about average. That's not too bad. Thank you so much."

"It's the least I could do. The Benway Moon Potato Chip company was looking to expand into the Crab Nebula anyway. And I think your poor parents deserve some good luck.

We're not always able to choose how our relatives behave."

"There she is!" shouted a familiar voice. "Johnny! She's over here!"

It was Verb. He had Johnny by the arm and was dragging him through the crowd of dancers in our direction.

"Hi, Theora! Johnny was looking for you. I helped him, because I thought you'd want to see him." He gave me a wink and grinned his big stupid grin. "You *do* want to see Johnny, don't you?"

There have been times in the past when I've wanted to strangle Verb, and there will probably be times in the future when I'll want to do the same thing. It's rare, though, that he deserves it as much as he did right then.

My little brother was probably saved by Tsam Saa arriving. "Excuse me, Miss Benway," he said. "Could I get a few minutes of your time for an interview? I just wanted to know what went through your mind when you were trapped in the Roach Motel."

"Certainly, but let's go outside where it's quiet." She nodded in my direction. "Beauty queens do not give interviews in discos. You remember that."

Tsam waved at me as they walked off. "*Thrilling Cockroach Tales* is going to love this," he said.

"Hey, that reminds me," said Claude to Eleven Evelyn. "Can I talk to you about getting a copy of the official bootleg of tonight's show?"

"I'll take you to the Minister of Bootlegs," she replied. "I know I just saw him around here somewhere."

That left Johnny, Verb, and me. Verb was still grinning.

After a long few seconds, Johnny took off his watch and handed it to my brother. "This watch has a hundred and eighty-seven different functions," he said. "If you can figure out half of them, you can have it."

"Really?" Verb's grin vanished, and he was no longer an obnoxious creep. He was just a little brother again, at least for right now.

"If you start levitating, float over to Melvin!" called Johnny, as Verb ran away. "He can fix it!"

"So," Johnny said, and laughed.

"So," I said, and laughed.

"I was going to ask you . . ." He trailed off and looked at his shoes.

"Yes?"

"Would you mind if I, um . . . Can I call you sometime?"

"That would be great," I said. I could feel my heart beating louder than the Moon Cockroach music. "Do you feel like dancing?"

"I do."

So did I. So we danced. It was a good night.

39

"I'm sorry, Miss Theremin, but it didn't seem very well researched. C-plus."

I was back at school, and Mrs. Vast was handing out our science project grades. Mrs. Vast was the substitute teacher the school had hired after Mr. Pinweed mysteriously disappeared. She was a better teacher, but she apparently didn't believe in Big Phil any more than Mr. Pinweed had.

I looked over my shoulder to where Ginger and Mary Beth were sitting. They shrugged at me.

After I had not only traveled to another planet and discovered an alien civilization but also found out the secret behind the Burger Buckaroo fast-food chain, it would seem like I'd have had tons of great material to make a science project, but that was not the case. On our trip back from Neptune, Dr. Übermind had gathered Verb, Ginger, Mary Beth, and me in the lounge of the Übermind rocket and sworn us to secrecy.

"I regret to say that the majority of Earth people are not quite ready to accept some of the things you've seen in the past few days," he said.

"Most people don't even know that the common desktop stapler has a rich and complex social life," added Johnny.

"For that reason, I must ask you to promise not to reveal what you have seen to any outside person," Dr. Übermind went on.

That was fine with me. After all, I was pretty sure no one would have believed me, even if I had wanted to tell. Mary Beth and Ginger agreed, too. It was easier for them, I think, since the effects of the Expositron ray had worn off a little bit, and their memories of Neptune were slightly fuzzy.

Verb was more of a problem. It wasn't that he wanted to go out and tell the world there were giant bugs serving hamburgers in cities across the country, but it just wasn't in his nature to keep quiet about things. After a serious talk from Dr. Übermind and a promise that he would appear in an upcoming Übermind Adventures book, Verb swore that he would do his best, but time will tell. I wouldn't bet on it.

We had stayed on Neptune for the final rounds of the Cavalcade of Loveliness, the day after the Moon Cockroaches' big party. To tell the truth, the other rounds weren't very exciting. After everything I had done since I got my first-round assignment, the rest—evening wear, swimwear, question-and-answer, laser gymnastics, and feats of strength —was all kind of tame.

I ended up getting third place, the prizes for which were

a small bronze tiara and a partial scholarship to the Planet Ixsvrong Institute of Technology, which I don't think I'll use. The runner-up was Miss Planet Thoo, who looked like a sort of silvery butterfly with stained-glass wings. She really was one of the most beautiful things I had ever seen, and I could understand why she'd been picked over me. The winner, the new Princess of Neptune, was Miss Planet Erb. She was the huge, motionless mound of blue fur that I had seen in line on my first day at Neptune, and she was from the same planet as the Cerulean Six. As her contestant wrangler had wheeled Miss Planet Erb forward in her red wagon to be crowned by Hortense Benway and the MC5000, Miss Planet Thoo must have noticed my shocked expression.

"I hear she had a *very* good swimsuit round," said Miss Planet Thoo.

There wasn't anything I could say to that, so I clapped and smiled as hard as anyone. I didn't really mind. I didn't think I was beauty queen material, to tell the truth. I was a lot more excited about the idea of recording an album, even if it would never be released on my own planet. I'd had fun being in the pageant, and I probably did pick up a few things about poise and confidence by watching Hortense Benway and the other contestants. As far as I was concerned, third place was fine.

This still doesn't explain why I ended up doing my science project on Big Phil, which was a pretty weak topic to begin with. I don't have a good excuse, really, except to say that I ran out of time. When we got back to Philodendron Landing with the Überminds, it took us a lot longer than we had expected to undo the damage that the Neptunian impostors, Two Hundred Marco and Seventy-four Tim, had done while they were pretending to be Ginger and Mary Beth. It turned out they weren't quite the masters of disguise that they claimed to be, and we had to straighten things out with the police, the people from the zoo, and everyone's families. But that's another story.

On top of that, Verb and I had to work out a cover story to explain what we had been doing while we were gone. Our parents were full of questions about Übermind Island, so we had to make sure that our stories didn't contradict each other. Then I had to deal with the dozens of phone calls from Hortense Benway's record company, trying to set up the best time to smuggle Mary Beth, Ginger, and me up to the moon so we could record the new album. At the moment, we're supposed to meet at the Burger Buckaroo at eight o'clock next Saturday morning, but this has already changed four times because of Hortense Benway's personal appearance schedule, so I'm not holding my breath.

By the time things had settled down and I realized I had to get to work on my science project, there were only two days left. I suppose I could have called Johnny and asked him to use all the resources of the Übermind Institute to put together something spectacular, but I didn't. I thought about it, but it felt like I would be taking advantage of him, so I went ahead with my original idea. Unfortunately, it turned out very much like what Mr. Pinweed had predicted: me sitting by the lake for a while, then writing a report that says "No monster." Still, it did get a C-plus. It could have been worse.

That afternoon, the Band with No Name was rehearsing in my parents' garage when the phone rang.

I jumped off the drum stool and picked up the cordless phone. "Hello?" I had brought it out because I was expecting a call from Johnny. Since Verb and I had never gotten to Übermind Island, we were going there over spring break, and Johnny and I had been calling back and forth, making plans.

"Hi!"

It wasn't Johnny.

"Hello, Verb."

"Guess where I'm calling from?"

"Just tell me," I said, not wanting to play this game.

"Burger Buckaroo!"

"Are you stuck there?" I asked. I imagined him cowering by the condiment dispenser, too scared to go out past the robotic mascot.

"No, it's not like that at all," Verb said. "I got a— Hey, wait a second!"

I heard some noises on the other end of the line, and a new voice came on.

"Dude!"

"Delaney!" I said. "Where are you?"

"Right down your street! We're the new managers of the Philodendron Landing Burger Buckaroo. Isn't that cool?"

Someone else took the phone. "Tsam pulled some strings and got us this job right before he left the corporation," said Harmonic Convergence.

"What happened to Tsam?"

"Didn't you hear? *Thrilling Cockroach Tales* liked his article so much that they hired him as their full-time beauty pageant correspondent. He'll be writing stories about all the big pageants now. In fact, he's on his way to the Most Perfect Protoplasm contest in Galactic Supercluster F33 as we speak."

That was great. A few days ago I had gotten a big envelope in the mail with a copy of *Thrilling Cockroach Tales* in it. It had a picture of Tsam and Hortense Benway on the cover, but the magazine was in Moon Cockroachese, so I couldn't read Tsam's article. I was glad to hear that things had worked out for him.

Now Verb was back on the phone. "The twins called me when they got into town and asked if I wanted to be their junior assistant salad bar technician. They usually don't hire human beings, you know, but they said they'd make an exception for me. I'm going to work for them after school and save up to buy an official Übermind radio telescope. The twins have been telling me all about the moon, and I want to see if I can pick up signals from Radio Bob."

"Verb, what about the mascot?" I asked. I couldn't imagine that he'd be brave enough to sneak past that giant hamburger every afternoon.

"It's okay, really," he said. He hesitated for a second. "Seriously. It's all right. Delaney and Harmonic Convergence are going to show me how it operates. They say I won't be scared if I know more about it."

"Do you think that will work?"

"If not, they said they'd reprogram it so it has to be nice to me," said Verb. "I'll be fine."

Behind me, Mary Beth and Ginger were waiting to rehearse the song we'd just written. It didn't have a title yet, but we were hoping to put it on Hortense Benway's new album.

I smiled. "Congratulations, Verb. I'm happy for you."